MELODY
BURNING

MELODY BURNING

BURNING

WHITLEY STRIEBER

Christy Ottaviano Books

Henry Holt and Company ★ New York

Henry Holt and Company, LLC
Publishers since 1866
175 Fifth Avenue
New York, New York 10010
macteenbooks.com

Library of Congress Cataloging-in-Publication Data
Strieber, Whitley.
Melody burning / Whitley Strieber.—1st ed.
p.   cm.
"Christy Ottaviano Books."
Summary: Melody, a sixteen-year-old celebrity living in an expensive
Hollywood high-rise with her manager-mother, meets a mysterious boy
who is determined to keep her safe.
ISBN 978-0-8050-9327-8 (hc)
[1. Apartment houses—Fiction.   2. Orphans—Fiction.
3. Criminals—Fiction.   4. Love—Fiction.   5. Hollywood (Los Angeles,
Calif.)—Fiction.   6. Los Angeles (Calif.)—Fiction.]   I. Title.
PZ7.S91675Me 2011   [Fic]—dc22   2011002863

First Edition—2011 / Book designed by Véronique Lefèvre Sweet
Printed in the United States of America

10 9 8 7 6 5 4 3 2 1

This book is dedicated to Anne Strieber,
who conceived it.

MELODY
BURNING

The construction elevator clattered and rattled as it sped them up higher and higher. The child clung to his father. It bothered him that the elevator had no walls, and he liked even less that it was moving fast, rising through the windy, dripping-wet skeleton of the building. He could see the sky out one side and girders rushing past on the other. The wind made the elevator rock. Its cables snapped and sang, and its motor whined. His dad held his hand tightly. The boy clutched the blue rose in his pocket. He took it everywhere. His mom had given it to him before she died. He believed that there was a secret string that started at the blue rose and ended in her hand in heaven.

"Will we be up in the clouds?"

Daddy laughed. "Nearly."

With a last clank, the elevator stopped.

Dad picked him up. "Now don't go anywhere near the edge, do you understand me? You could blow right off in this wind. I'm gonna take some pictures, and if anybody comes up here, what did I tell you to say?"

"My daddy brought me here to see how high it was."

"And did your daddy take any pictures?"

He shook his head. "Just one of me."

Dad hugged him. "That's right."

He pulled open the big plywood door with the number 50 and the word TOP spray-painted on it. "Top of the world," he said, "highest point in Los Angeles."

They got out onto the wet roof. The storm had left puddles, and the sweeping wind rippled the surface of them. There were places where you could see through to the floors below and down for what seemed like miles. Gulls screamed in the dark, rushing clouds, white against surging gray. He had learned about gulls in school.

Dad stood him beside a big plywood shack. "Don't move unless I tell you." He stepped back and took a picture of him.

"Can I see it?"

"Later."

"How high are we?"

"High enough. Don't move from that spot. Is that understood?"

"Yes, Daddy." Since Mommy had gone to heaven, he had learned to follow Daddy and always obey him.

It was cold here, and all of a sudden it was really lonely, because Daddy had gone into a room on the far side of the roof. Through the partially open door, he could see camera flashes.

Then he saw a man in a dark coat, shining with rain. The man did not see him at first. He was looking intently toward the flashes.

The flashes continued, and the man went closer.

He was a small man, not huge like Daddy. His face was white and pinched, his eyes narrow slits.

The man said, "Come outta there."

The flashes stopped.

Then the boy saw that the man was carrying a gun. It was black and shiny and pointing straight into the room where Daddy was.

Daddy had said not to move from this spot, but Daddy had not said that there would be somebody with a gun. So the boy looked around for a place to hide.

"Luther," Daddy said as he came out of the room, "you can't do this. I can't allow it."

"You don't have any right to be up here. You're trespassing."

"This structure is full of violations, Luther. It's a death—" Daddy stopped talking. He looked down at the gun. "It's a death trap, Luther!"

The man Daddy was calling Luther gestured with the gun. "Give me the camera."

"You can't be serious. Put that damn thing away!"

Daddy sounded scared, and that made the boy's heart start beating hard.

"You gonna give me that camera?"

"Hell, no."

"Yeah, you are."

"What're you gonna do, Luther, shoot me?"

The man turned. His eyes were like knives. "C'mere, kid."

"Robbie, *no*!"

The man came closer, and Robbie backed away, but suddenly the man was right there, his fist closed around Robbie's shirt, and he picked him up. Robbie fought and kicked, but the man was strong, and all of a sudden, he was holding him out over the edge.

"Oh, God. Oh, God. Luther, no!"

"Give me the camera!"

"Okay! Jesus, man, his shirt's tearing!"

Robbie could see the ground way, way down, and he could feel his shirt sliding up. He looked at the man, and the man's face was funny, his eyes widening.

"JESUS, LUTHER!"

He slipped. Then Daddy was there. Daddy was looking down at him, his hands coming, and Robbie was slipping—and then Daddy yelled and grabbed him and Robbie flew up and over onto the roof—and somebody was screaming, and the scream faded away fast.

Then Robbie was on the roof, and the man was on the roof, but Daddy was gone.

The man stared at him, eyes flicking from side to side, and he grabbed for him, but Robbie ran as fast as he could. The man roared and followed, but Robbie went into the room where Daddy had been. It was dark, and there were wires and pipes, and he went behind them. When the man came in, Robbie went down between two of the pipes and then was in a dark space.

Robbie crawled into the space. The man called to him, screamed that he would shoot Robbie, so Robbie kept going deeper into the dark, narrow space.

After a while, the man stopped calling. Then Robbie heard the elevator going down.

Still, he did not move.

Gradually, the light faded. The gulls stopped screaming. Night scared him, and so he still did not move. How long he slept he did not know. But the next day, nobody came. It was getting late, and he came out onto the roof. Slowly, his heart hammering, he went to the edge and looked down. Daddy was down there, and he was dead, and that hurt Robbie's soul and scared him more than anything, because now what did he do? Where did he go?

He was hungry, and he wanted orange juice, but there was nothing here. He could not go down—he didn't dare—and anyway he had no idea how to make the elevator come. There was no button, just a lever that he couldn't reach.

Night came again, and he found a place near the pipes that was a little warm. He sat close to the pipes and cried. He cried hard and long. Then he heard the elevator. He stopped crying. Maybe somebody was coming to help him. Maybe somebody would take him somewhere, and he would tell about the man, and they would find a place for him to live and give Daddy a beautiful funeral like Mommy had, with all the flowers.

But that made his heart hurt.

The elevator rattled and clattered, getting louder and louder.

Then it stopped. The door scraped open . . . but nobody came out. Then someone did—and at first he didn't understand what he was seeing: a black, hunched figure with a weird robot face.

He choked back a scream, watching as the figure looked carefully around the roof. When it faced in his direction, he saw the gleaming glass eyes of a robot—but then the thing's arms reached up and the robot face came off. It wasn't a face at all; it was a mask and it glowed inside with green light, and the green light revealed the real face of the person who had been wearing it.

The man was back again.

Robbie stopped breathing. He was a small mass of pure fear . . . and hate. He had never known this emotion before, and he had no word for it, but he wished on his blue rose that the man would just die.

Then the man put the mask back on and went stalking off across the roof. He was hunting for Robbie, and Robbie knew what would happen when he was found: he would be thrown off the roof, too. And that mask was not a mask—it was a thing that made you able to see in the dark. He'd seen those on TV.

As the man came closer to the hiding place, Robbie wished that he could jump out and push him off the roof. But the man was too big.

He stopped. He looked this way. Slowly, he began walking toward Robbie's hiding place.

Robbie was hypnotized by the oncoming figure. His mouth went dry. His heart fluttered. He wanted to cry, but his fear was so great that he grew stiff and silent, unable to make a sound.

The man came right up to him . . . but he didn't look down, not far enough, not to this dark corner.

The man crept around for a long, long time, moving from one end of the roof to the other, looking in every nook and cranny. But he never found the small boy lodged in a corner of the equipment shed.

Finally, the man went away. Sometime the next day, the boy heard distant sirens, and for a while he thought somebody would come save him, but nobody ever did. He watched the light of day rise and then fall, and he watched the sun slip into the Pacific Ocean.

Only then did he come out onto the windy roof. He took out his silk rose and held it in both hands up to the starry sky. He asked his mom and his dad to come get him and take him up there, too.

He jumped toward the stars, but he couldn't make it more than a few inches. Again he jumped, and again.

Then he cried. He went in the equipment shed, where it was warmer, and he cried until he fell asleep.

The next morning the building filled up with workmen. Still, he hid in the back of the equipment room.

When he could, he crept out and took food from the workers' lunch boxes. He ate sandwiches and drank Cokes, and another day passed. When it was dark, he climbed to the highest point on the building and held up his rose and waited.

He waited until he was too cold and then he went back to the equipment shed. It had changed. Now there were big motors in it. He could get behind the motors and hide really well.

Another day passed, and many more, and he lost count of

the days. He lived in the dark, in the recesses of the building, which he heard being called the Beresford.

Sometimes he saw Luther. His hate was a nasty feeling, and he didn't like it, but he couldn't help it.

All he had left of his old life was his blue rose. He would see his mom and his dad in its petals. Eventually, he gave up waiting for them to come down from heaven for him.

The building got built, people moved in, and he went from eating workers' lunches to sneaking into kitchens.

As time passed, he forgot where he came from, how old he was, Mom's name, Dad's name, even his own name. So he gave himself a new one.

He called himself Beresford.

CHAPTER 1

I hear you, I know I do.
Who are you?
Who are you?
Don't scare me, don't hurt me,
Don't go, don't go, don't go....

This is a really beautiful building and all, but something is wrong here. I don't know what it is yet, but it's starting to kind of piss me off. Maybe it should scare me, I don't know. Right now I'm in my bedroom on the fiftieth floor, and it sounds like somebody's in the stairwell behind my wall.

There are three doors to this apartment—the kitchen door, the front door, and the den door. The den is here at the end of the apartment, next to my room. Through its door is the back stairwell for movers and things.

Could it be somebody working back there? No, not at this hour.

A stalker?

Oh, man, these guys, there are so many of them.

Last night, I got Mom in here to listen. The verdict? The wind making the building sway. Tonight there is no wind, and I'm once again hearing this, so, *hello?* Except I know I can't prove it to her, not unless I actually catch somebody. She's going to come down on me again about a shrink, and I don't want that because prescriptions will follow, and that is a road that only goes down.

Mom thinks teens should be messy and chaotic, and I'm anything but, so her theory is that I'm too tense. She's the one who's too tense, and her part of our world is complete bedlam.

Anyway, with this life I'm living, I'm totally tired all the time, so maybe it's just my wild imagination. But how do you sleep with paranoia?

My concert's coming up, and half the songs aren't even written. Plus, I'm behind memorizing my lines for *Swingles*. Plus, Sandy Green assigned me over a hundred pages of *Middlemarch* for our English class. Thank you so much. (You think it would be cool to be a showbiz kid with a tutor and no formal classes? Believe me, it's not cool. You can cut classes, but try cutting your tutor. Ain't gonna happen.)

I'm at the point in my career where it's either going up or going down, so I *have* to be awesome in every episode of *Swingles*, no matter how tired I am, and I absolutely must fill the Greek Theatre to capacity when my concert happens. I mean, that old outdoor theater in Griffith Park is part of LA music history. Tina Turner, David Bowie, and Elton John performed there, among many others. Getting a gig at the Greek really, really matters.

So I don't exactly need distractions. I pick up my guitar, start hunting for a melody. But what if this person is sitting out there listening? Can he hear me? I don't want him to hear me.

Mom moved us here because the Beresford is ultimate glitz, and right now I need high-profile everything. Paparazzi don't do dinky condos in Calabasas.

Anyway, it's okay because downtown LA is good. There are clubs like M&M where I can just walk in despite being under-age, and nobody cares. The line claps when I get out of my car. Mike and Mikey, who own the place, are jaw-to-the-floor over me. I think they'd pay me to chill there all the time.

I don't have a boyfriend because when you turn into a celebrity as fast as I have, dating gets complicated. I dance by myself, and usually when I stop, I'm alone in the middle of a sea of cell phone cameras. I don't care. My own heart is my best dancing partner anyway.

I have Julius, my bodyguard. Julius wears a suit to remind everybody that he is with me on a professional basis. If I want a guy to keep hitting on me, I have to give Julius a little three-fingered wave. Otherwise, the guy is swept away. Zoom.

Gone. Then later you see him looking sheepish at the bar or whatever.

Stuff like this is probably why I really enjoy being alone, like right now when I'm in my room with the city out there sparkling in the night.

Except, am I alone?

I haven't heard the sound for a while, so maybe it is really nothing. The wind making the building sway.

I fool around with my guitar. My guitar is my most private place. And yet, it's also my link to my fans and to the world.

I find a melody, it's sweet, it has a catch in it. Nice. So I sing, "I hear you, I know I do. Who are you? Who are you?"

I'm not gonna call Julius, and I'm not gonna wake up Mom, but I need to get past feeling there is someone watching me.

I press my ear against the wall.

Nothing. So am I alone or not?

I put on the new billowy robe Mom gave me. I get the black and red can of Mace out of the drawer in my bedside table. Julius has taught me how to use it. I put my finger through the ring.

If there is some guy out there, I'm going to spray him like the roach that he is. *Then* I'll tell Mom. *Then* I will call Julius. Nobody is gonna tell me it's the damn wind.

Okay, I open my door. I step out into the hall. The apartment is really quiet—but not completely dark. As I look down the hall and across the living room, I see a faint line of light under Mom's door on the far side. She's awake. Also, I hear music. Frank Sinatra. So I know who's in there with her: Dapper Dan. At least, that's what I call him. She's dating two guys, Dapper D, who wears sports jackets and takes her to hear cabaret, and the Wolverine. He looks like an Egyptian mummy trying to be an Elvis impersonator and likes to go clubbing. Faint music drifts through the apartment.

Furious as she makes me, my heart hurts for my mom. Bottom line, my dad ditched her for a bimbo. We fight all the time, but I'll never leave her or stop loving her. It breaks my heart to see how hard she tries to find her way out of the loneliness of her life. But she's a pistol.

I turn. Now I'm facing the window at the far end of this hall. To my left is the door into the den. I enter it.

This is where all my books are. My poetry book that Daddy read to me when I was little. "The old canoe by the shadowy shore . . ." I would sit cuddled in his arms. We had a nice life, I thought. Guess nobody was happy except me.

Okay, the door is right over there. All I have to do is unlock it and step out into the stairwell. Oh, God, I am so scared. Mom's room is far away. I could scream but she'd never believe me. And *Mace*? What if it doesn't work, or I spray myself? What if he has a gun?

I put a hand on the bolt and, as silently as possible, I turn it. There is the faintest of scrapes.

My song echoes in my mind. "I hear you, I know I do, I know I do . . ."

Vampire?

Don't go there, girl. Anyway, they don't exist.

Ghost?

I lean against the door. The silence from the other side is total.

So maybe it is a ghost.

And then I feel the door move. As in, somebody just leaned against it from the other side. *Pushing*.

The second I turn the knob, they're going to burst in on me.

Very slowly, very quietly, I turn the bolt back . . . only it won't go back—it's stuck. Because he's out there pushing so hard the door is warping.

He must be incredibly strong. He must be huge.

And he knows I'm here, and he's just an inch away.

I twist the bolt harder . . . and finally it clicks in.

The whole door creaks. Then it sort of lets go. Has he moved away? Was he even there?

I am about to be sick. I want to say "I have a gun," but I can't make my throat work.

I run back into my room, lock my door, and dive into bed. I clutch the Mace like it's a lifeline.

And now, another sound against the wall. I hate this! I can't stand this! Am I losing my mind for real?

I look at the phone. If I pick it up and call Julius, he'll be up here in five minutes with ten cops trailing behind. Except I just wish I could prove there really is a guy out there and it's not all in my head. Because it could be. I fear that.

I get out of bed and pick up my guitar.

> *I hear you, I know I do.*
> *Who are you?*
> *Who are you?*
> *Don't scare me, don't hurt me,*
> *Don't go, don't go, don't go....*

Am I completely insane to even sing that? Except it's got flow. It does. I click on Voice Memo on my iPad and do it again. Let the songs come.

Real songs come out of hurt and loss and longing. If they also come out of fear, then this is a winner.

I close my eyes, imagining who I used to be. Melanie Cholworth. Melody McGrath is much better—I have to admit Mom is right about that. Nowadays, I have to actually pretend that I'm the real me. I guess Melody took over.

I get back into bed and close my eyes. But sleep doesn't come; sleep is far away. Even though it's quiet now, I can't stop listening. I imagine claws coming through the wall.

On the day we moved in and I arrived with my gaggle of snapping paparazzi, I looked up at the soaring facade and I had this gut reaction that made me go, "Ohmygosh."

In my mind's eye, I saw people tumbling off the balconies. . . . They were all girls about my age, and they all had my hair and my complexion and my clothes on, and they were all falling just like I think I would probably fall, with their arms spread wide, trying to say "I am flying, Mother dear—look at me!"

Fly and fly and fly and fly. . . . There's a song there, girl, remember that. Songs live in my nooks and crannies. I have to hunt for them like a miner looking for diamonds or whatever, I guess.

Shit! I hear it again.

No way am I staying in my room, but also no way am I going to Mom's room when she and Dapper D might be getting cozy.

So I drag the mattress, which turns out to be really heavy, until it's all the way across the room.

I look at my wall. How thick is it? Could he cut his way through?

I will sing all night, until the dawn. Trouble is, dawn's so far away and I am so alone.

CHAPTER 2

Deep in the Beresford's basement, Frank the Torch listened, and he didn't like what he was hearing. This was exactly what Mr. Szatson had complained about. Some squatter. "Get him outta there, Frank. Wylie couldn't do it, but you know your way around buildings. Get him out." Wylie had been his predecessor. Fired over the squatter. Or so it appeared.

Six weeks ago, he'd come off a nickel in San Quentin two years early. Why the sentence reduction he did not know, but he was not about to argue. He'd been in for a dumb little job in City of Industry, the Alert Cleaners fire. The owner was looking to cash out and retire and couldn't find a buyer, so he'd called Frank. It had been an easy job—ten bills in his wallet, don't even think about it.

Except he'd come up against a control-freak insurance investigator who'd found an image of him on the security camera tape of the gas station across the street. With his record, it was a no-brainer. The jury took nineteen minutes to convict.

As soon as he was out, he'd gotten a call on his cell: Mr. Szatson wants to see you. He'd known Szatson for years, for the same reason that he knew a lot of real estate developers. They needed fires, these guys, and arson was Frank's profession. Also, he was at the top of the heap when it came to skills. He'd been a civil engineer, so he knew structures. If you hired him, you could count on three things: The fire would work. The arson investigators would not trace it back to you. You would get your payday.

Mr. Szatson had sent him to work at the Beresford as its superintendent. "You're an engineer, Frank. I need an engineer. Because the place has problems. There's a squatter and a lot of famous and rich tenants. I don't need that crap, so I want you to get rid of him."

There were lots of ways to hide in a big place like this. Too many.

He didn't think that was the only reason he'd been hired, though. Maybe Szatson had even pulled him out of the stir. He was that powerful. To put it bluntly, Szatson needed a fire. Somewhere in the Szatson empire, Frank the Torch was going to do a job, and probably more than one. Not here, though. This was the Szatson flagship.

Frank was thrilled by the Beresford. Aside from making sure the heat worked and the elevators didn't get stuck, there wasn't a lot to do but watch the beautiful people come and go. There were stars in the place, Melody McGrath, for instance. Pretty as a picture, sweet as honey. But that mother of hers—wow, that was one power hitter. He'd never tangled with her, but he'd been warned by other members of the staff that she was a bullmastiff and you did not want to cross her.

You also did not want her to pull her precious daughter out of the place since she brought so much media attention. If anything went wrong, they would surely leave.

He flipped from one security camera to the next. He'd seen this character—glimpsed him—standing in front of the laundry room. Black clothes, head to foot. Wild hair.

He was going to find him and take him somewhere far away. Maybe even drop the bastard off a cliff. Or at least punch him out.

CHAPTER 3

I went through today like a zombie and made everybody on the *Swingles* set furious. Mom thinks I'm hallucinating or whatever, and here I am alone in my room and *I just heard it again*! This time it went *hisss*, not like a snake but as if it was sliding against my wall.

Sleep is once again not an option, so I'm gonna work. The *Swingles* call is at six thirty tomorrow, and I could memorize my lines now instead of in the limo at the crack of dawn like I did this morning.

Swingles is pretty fun, actually. The pilot was huge in the ratings, and then came better news: the second week didn't bring all that much ratings deterioration, as they call it.

I'm lying on my right side and facing my wall of glass, letting my eyes slowly close to LA at night with a slice of moon above. Very beautiful and mysterious, as long as you don't think about the fact that the city is really a sea of condos and strip malls.

While I'm lying here thinking of the mysteries of life and wondering if love will ever come my way (I'm such a drama queen), the sound comes and I jump off the bed.

After a moment, the sliding starts again.

Is it coming from the other side of the wall, or inside it?

I grab my laptop and go to the Beresford's website, where I pull up the apartment layouts. (Can we *really* afford eleven grand a month for this amazing apartment?)

Anyway, my bedroom backs onto a service shaft beside the stairwell outside our den.

So maybe Mom is sort of right. But it's not the building swaying—it's projected sound from somewhere coming up through the shaft behind my room or the stairwell behind that.

So here's a creepy thought: what if what I'm hearing is somebody actually cutting through the wall, not from the stairwell but from inside the shaft beside it? I've already had about forty-seven stalkers, guys with dirty T-shirts and gray skin and hunter's eyes.

If you had a gun, you could shoot me right through the

wall that's behind the headboard of my bed. While I was on the *Swingles* set today, the maid put my bed back together. Maybe I'll move the mattress again.

Jesus—I am so neurotic, which is why my insides are turning into an acid bath. I'm sixteen and already chug Mylanta. Xanax is next, then amitriptyline, then up the line through Prozac to the Effexors of the world. I know the drill.

Maybe there is no .357 Magnum out there an inch from my headboard. Maybe it's something innocent but annoying, like a papi trying to plant a spike camera. If you don't know what that is, it looks just like a nail. Stick it through a wall, and you've got an eye in the room. Add a spike mike, and your target is in a movie.

What if it's some horrible old man who lives in the basement and comes up at night? What if he isn't a vampire but a cannibal? Has anybody ever disappeared in this place?

You're sixteen years old, girl, and *there's no bogeyman here.* Oh, my dear Beresford that I must now call home, you are haunted by a very real *something.*

I listen. Breathing? Maybe. Or maybe it's that I'm insane. That's what Mom would think.

Quiet time of the night, everybody asleep except me. Is somebody in with Mom? Don't know. Instead of looking, this time I just lock my door. I take my Mace out and cradle it.

Earlier, I reread the instructions. Pull the ring and press the red button. It's pretty simple, actually.

If a shot came through the wall, would I even have a second to realize I was dying?

I know he's out there.

Except now he's quiet. So maybe it's something else. I close my eyes and let my music take my mind.

"Far and far and far and far, I'm going far and far and far and far, and the stars are way behind me, the stars are way behind me."

I sleep with my head at the foot of the bed and all my pillows piled up against the wall to cushion the bullets.

CHAPTER 4

He could hear her; she was singing, and he pressed against the wall, listening to her voice—"far and far and far and far . . ." And he was so close to her, but also far and far and far.

Before Melody, he had looked at girls and liked girls, but now there was this huge difference. Seeing her for the first time had caused an explosion inside him. He had no idea that feelings like this existed. Sure, he'd seen girls, plenty of them, but never one who glowed like Melody McGrath, whose hair seemed filled with the sun, whose eyes laughed and said "come here," whose skin looked as soft as the air itself.

He hadn't known that you could feel this way, and he wasn't sure if it meant that he was okay or that he was not okay.

He had to be near her. But he must never let her see him. Leaving this shaft where he was practically living now was too hard for him. He'd never known anything like the desire that kept him pressed up here against the drywall, listening to every faint sound from her room on the other side and holding an image of her in his mind.

He could see the gleam of her eyes, the broad paleness of her forehead, the way her lips seemed to laugh gently, as if she possessed some secret knowledge.

All of this he'd watched on *Swingles*. His love affair—for that's what it was, even if he did not understand it—had started when he'd been watching the show one evening in some vacationer's apartment.

A bristling shock had shot through him when he recognized her as one of the new people here in the Beresford and also realized that she was the most beautiful girl on earth.

Immediately, he'd climbed the chase, or shaft, up to an apartment whose tenants used their TiVo a lot, slipped in through his hatch, and added *Swingles* to their queue. Now when they were gone, he could watch. And he did, over and over again, loving her, longing for her with a pain at once sweeter and sharper than any he knew, except when he held the blue rose.

More than once, the thought of going in there had crossed his mind. He was afraid, though. He did not like her mother's voice; it had a knife in it.

He was much too shy to ever look at a girl changing or in

the shower or anything like that. He tried not to go into the same apartment too often. Except for Mrs. Scutter's—to be sure she wasn't setting her bed on fire with a cigarette. She'd done that once, and since then he made sure to check on her every night.

When he imagined being with Melody, it was in the nicest place he knew, which was the park he could see far below. Trees and flowers bloomed there in summertime, and if he listened closely, he could hear music playing and kids yelling in happy voices.

He'd looked at himself in mirrors in the bathrooms of vacancies and vacationers. Wasn't he kind of odd looking? Every day, his nose got bigger, it seemed to him. And he cut his hair as best he could, but it was still too shaggy. He wanted to look like other guys, not like some kind of freak.

His dad, he remembered, had short hair, and he thought he should have it, too. He barely remembered Mom, except that she had wavy blond hair like Melody, and she laughed, and she had given him his blue rose.

He thought Melody was about his age, but he wasn't really sure. How old was he, anyway?

Now he was in the equipment shaft—called Chase Two during construction—beside Melody's bedroom. It was making him happy and sad at the same time to hear her in there. Earlier, she'd moved her bed so she was no longer so close that he could listen to her voice and her guitar.

Then he heard another sound, one that instantly drew his attention: a high, mournful sound like wind sweeping around the corner of the building. It was coming, he knew, from ten floors below, drifting up the chase from 4021.

Gilford was crying. This was because Tommy was out late again, and Gilford cried then. Tommy had no idea how much Gilford loved him.

He wanted to stay here near Melody, but he had a job to do, so he grasped the edge of one of the girders that framed the chase and quickly dropped down the ten floors, pulsing his fingers along the pipes, letting himself slide just fast enough but not so fast that he would lose control. The dark hole that yawned below hardly mattered to him. Falling was hard to imagine. When he was little, though, he'd fallen some—never more than a story or two.

When he felt himself dropping, he'd let himself go loose. That way it didn't hurt too much, but he knew he couldn't withstand stories and stories.

He arrived at forty and went along the crawl space to Tommy's apartment. He was growing, so the crawl spaces were getting smaller. He wasn't fat; he was just, well, big. Dad had been really, really huge, so maybe he would be huge, too. Then what happened? Without the ability to use his crawl spaces . . . he didn't even want to think about it.

He reached Tommy's apartment and went over to where

he had installed his hatch. Over the years, he'd built lots of hatches. People thought they were supposed to be there.

He wanted to be where Melody was, to be her friend, to sit on the couch together. In a whisper in his mind, he told himself the same story again and again. He was with Melody on the couch. He said to her, "I love you," and she turned to him, and that wonderful smile came across her face, and then their lips touched.

Oh, yeah, like that would happen. He wanted to at least just breathe the air in her apartment. He wanted to, but he was scared because—well, the way she made him feel was just scary, with his whole body shivering like it did. As he slid open his hatch into Tommy's, Gilford was already whining at the door of the little foyer closet it opened into. He dropped down, pushing back Tommy's rarely used winter jackets, then opened the door.

He stepped into the foyer and immediately listened to the apartment while Gilford wiggled. He could hear slow breathing coming from the bedroom. That would be Annabelle. The breaths were regular and long. She was sound asleep.

He needed to be really careful here. He had not expected Annabelle to be home while Tommy was out.

Bending down, he let Gilford lick his face. The dog was a mass of wiggles.

"Hey, Gilly," he whispered. "Hey, bud." Gilford was a pug.

That's what Tommy told people he was, a pug. He had a pushed-in face and he snorted a lot, but he was very sweet.

As Beresford went through to the living room, Gilford trotted with him, his nose in the air. He knew that it was treat and cuddle time because that's what they both liked. But in the middle of the living room, Beresford stopped and listened carefully again. Annabelle had nearly caught him once. Just by nature, she was very quiet.

He headed for the kitchen, Gilford capering beside him, jumping up on his jeans. Or rather, Marty Prince's jeans. Beresford's clothes were all borrowed from tenants' closets.

Tommy did not have one of the most wonderful kitchens in the building. For great kitchens, you needed the older people like Helen Dooling. She cooked chicken and made pie.

He had learned to eat just a little here and a little there, never much in any one apartment.

"So, what we got?" he whispered to Gilford as he peered into the fridge, looking at the food arrayed on the shelves.

He fed Gilford some milk.

Then he heard the telltale sound of the elevator door opening. Somebody getting out on forty—no way he could take a chance. So he took Gilford's face in his hands and gave him a quick nose smooch and went back to the foyer closet.

The key clattered in the lock. Continuing to lift himself, his heart hammering, Beresford slipped into the crawl space and carefully closed his hatch.

He wanted to race up the chase, but he forced himself not to make a sound.

Moving slowly at first, climbing hand over hand, he made his way back up to fifty, back to his station behind Melody's wall. Through the thin plasterboard, he could hear her breathing softly and steadily.

Sleep, little angel, for I will watch over you.

CHAPTER 5

I'm goin' far and far and far and far
Up past the trees and the sky and the stars.
Far and far and far and far,
Where it's soft forever, soft and blue, soft and blue,
And I can reach out, and I can touch you
Far and far and far and far.

The set is blazing hot, and I'm dying. Thank heavens Ted the Elf called a break. (That's my own private nickname for our tiny, hoppity director.) Now I'm in my trailer, where I'm supposed to have a little peace and quiet, but Mom is screaming at Mark, my manager, over the fact that *Swingles* isn't using my music in the dance sequences.

Mom says into her phone, "We have to do this, Mark. We need the exposure! Plus, it's in her contract.... *Why not?* She's the star—it can only help the show! ... So what's he doing? Does he have another ingenue in the wings? Some tramp, Linda Lady or somebody?"

Linda Lady is my competition—sort of. She's all electronics, though. She can't actually sing, so she's gonna do a concert sooner or later that reveals she's lip-synching. There will be no forgiveness.

Mom paces, she makes a whistling sound through the plastic cigarette she uses whenever she is near me, and all of a sudden I feel this amazing love for her. She tries *so hard*. If we go down, it's not just going to break her heart—it's going to break her totally.

There's a knock. Mom looks at the door like a rabbit looks at a wolf, but it's only Thor Bradford, my acting coach.

Thor comes in. He appraises me, his eyes taking in every detail. He grins and twiddles his fingers at Mom, who takes this as her cue to leave us alone in the trailer.

As she goes out, she crushes the plastic cigarette to pieces in an ashtray. By the time the door closes, she's already back on her BlackBerry. She's calling for the box office overnights. The question every afternoon is the same: How is the Greek filling? What if I have to play to a half house? Or if I have to make up an excuse and cancel? "Miss McGrath has sprained her elbow and cannot perform." Behind every excuse like that lies the same reality: empty seats.

These are dangerous times for any performer, especially somebody like me, just building an audience.

Thor asks me, "Honey, do you have a problem with Alex?"

"No." (That is to say, YES!)

"Because on the dailies, we're seeing you kind of bend away

from him when he tries to kiss you. Like he smells bad. Not like you wish he'd follow through."

"I thought I was supposed to be unsure. It says in the script, 'unsure.'"

Then Thor takes me in his arms and says, "My Tic Tac loves your Tic Tac!" (Yes, the show is stupid. And yes, it's full of product placements. They have to make money, and anyway I actually *do* like Tic Tacs.)

I lean back—but then he stage kisses me. This is not a real kiss, but it looks like one. You keep your mouths closed. It's very clinical feeling. So I melt into it. I try to imagine that this elderly gay acting coach is the guy who never quite comes into focus in my dreams.

"Now, that's good. That's what we want to see."

"But Alex doesn't kiss me in the script."

As Thor leaves, he says over his shoulder, "Oh, that's changed. He kisses you now."

"It'd better be a stage kiss."

"Not my problem, beautiful." He leaves, and I go to the fridge, crack a Diet Coke mini, and chug it. I have to face facts: I just plain loathe Alex Steen. Loathe, loathe, loathe. Not only does he smell weird, he has skin like some kind of an amphibian. Maybe he's a skink.

I shouldn't be repulsed by him when half the girls in America would like to jump him, but I can't help how I feel.

"You're wanted on set."

"Thanks, Michael."

Michael is Ted's personal assistant. He's about twenty-two and starting out on the ground floor. I'm always polite and thankful to him. Mom doesn't even know his name.

As I go across the street to the soundstage where our set is, I see Mom huddled over her BlackBerry like it's a bird she's captured. Her back is to me. Whatever she's talking about, she's hiding it from the world, which makes me feel kind of sick inside because it can't be good or she'd be all over me, whispering good news as she listened to it coming in.

"Hey, sugar," Alex calls to me.

He's been told not to call me this by the network's political correctness maven, but he does it anyway.

I smile as mechanically as I can. Bright fake grin that's a clue he chooses to ignore.

For this scene, we're in the living room set. There's a couch, chairs, and a flat-screen TV that's really just a prop. When you see something on it in the background during the show, that's the special effects department. The whole set is like that. Even the chairs are so light you could throw them. The window is a breakaway (it's made out of melted sugar). We used it two episodes ago. In the scene, Mr. Forbes shattered it when his upper bridge flew out of his mouth and hit it. (Our writers apparently think that escaping dental prosthetics are funny.)

"Places, please. Is everyone aware of our changes?"

Nobody says anything. We're all afraid of Ted. He doesn't exactly carry a horsewhip like directors supposedly did in the past. Instead, he whips with sarcasm.

Ted gives me a long look. I feel like a butterfly about to be pinned. "She's SHINY!"

That brings a distant crash, and a couple of seconds later, a huge figure looms past the window and comes around the edge of the set. This is Martin, and he powders my immense forehead yet again. Shine is a no-no, but I'm not sure exactly why. I mean, I'm sixteen years old and therefore an oil factory, right?

So we take our positions, and Ted says "action," and all of a sudden I'm not Melody or even Melanie anymore. I'm Babsie, and I'm full of flutters because Seth—that's Alex—wants to kiss me and we're at my house and my dad is suspicious of him. Last week, when I brought Seth home for the first time, Dad asked to see his driver's license. Dad is out back cooking steaks, though, and Mom is in the kitchen, so this is Seth's chance.

Ted moves his hands, encouraging me. I'm supposed to flutter at Seth, which I do.

Seth paces in front of the fireplace. He looks at me. His eyes look kind of odd, actually.

The way the scene works, Seth kisses me, Dad comes in with the steaks, and Seth panics and jumps out the window.

I sit and turn into Babsie. I look down, sort of smiling. Babsie wants this—she wants Seth to just hurry up and do it.

So Seth takes a step closer. And another. I say my line: "I think you've got something on your cheek." I smile and pat the place beside me. "Come on, let me look."

Seth trips over the coffee table, which collapses. (It's balsa.) Frantically, he tries to put it together again. I say, "Dad's not gonna like that."

He stares at me like I'm totally insane, and there it is again, that weird look in his eyes—vacant. He's not Seth at all, he's Alex all the way, and he makes my blood run cold.

Now the kiss. I say, "Oh, Seth."

He grabs me and embraces me, and here it comes—but his mouth is *not* closed like it's supposed to be. He is into this; he's kissing me for real.

I'm furious. Ted needs to control Alex. Now he's pushing against me and jamming his face into mine, then we go off the couch and I hear Ted somewhere in some other universe yelling, while Alex keeps at me, and I can't get out from under him; he's like some kind of machine made of iron.

I have so many dreams of guys, but not *this* one—this is the nightmare that no girl ever wants to think about, and it's happening to me right in the middle of a television studio filled with people.

Stop him, somebody!

And then there are voices, shouting, Ted's voice above them all as he shouts himself crazy. The weight is gone, Alex is off, and Ted and our assistant director, Sam Dine, are holding him. But he's like some kind of animal, and they almost can't keep him under control. His eyes are really scary.

I get up, and Mom is there. She puts a towel around me, and I realize my blouse is all torn up, but at least it's just my costume.

Ted is in Alex's face. They stare each other down. Then Ted turns away, disgusted. "He's high," he says to Sam Dine. Then, louder, "We'll move into the kitchen. Thirty minutes—get it lit!" The kitchen scene is me and Mom and Dad, no Seth. More quietly, he tells Sam, "Whatever it takes, bring him down. And find whatever it is he's using and get it the hell off the lot."

I am sick to my stomach, trying to hold it in, and all I can think of is my trailer. I knew this would happen, I just knew it. He's always icked me out, and now I know why. I'm not a smoker or a drinker. A lot of kids at Calabasas High smoked, and there was every kind of drug you might want there, mostly prescripts, though. Not whatever *this* is, which is probably something harder.

On the way to the trailer, a papi I know named Brandon Carcelli comes out of nowhere from between my trailer and the wall of the soundstage, and his camera starts clicking away.

Fury like actual fire just explodes in my head, and I break away from Mom and go after him. He runs, I run, I am screaming at him, he turns and shoots, runs more, turns and shoots, and I know I'm getting into trouble, but I can't help myself. I am just so mad.

Then security is there, and he's soon surrounded and hustled off the lot.

Mom runs up. "Come on, honey, you're falling out."

Well, not quite, but my blouse is ripped and there's bra showing.

"How did he get in here, Mom?"

She shakes her head. "Look in the wallets at the gate. Carcelli probably paid his way in."

My trailer is quiet and cool, and I go in the bathroom and gargle Listerine until I feel sort of clean. Sort of.

"I want Alex fired," I say to Mom. "I never want him near me again!" I'm shocked to hear the rage in my voice. I think of myself as mild and nice, and I know that I've gone deeper into celebrity. I will wreck Alex's career because he went too far with me. But he deserves it—he's totally out of control.

I want to cry. I've never been kissed much before, and in the celebrity bubble where I live now, finding a normal boy probably will never happen for me.

Ted and Mark and Sam come in, and suddenly the trailer feels like a funeral. And maybe that's just what it is.

Mom talks for me. I have nothing to say about anything, it seems. Even though it was me this happened to.

"Mel, we need to be very careful," Ted says to me. His voice is different from the usual.

Mom says, "We understand that, Ted."

Their eyes meet, and do I see daggers? What's happening that I'm not being filled in on?

"Legal will have to get involved," Ted says.

There is silence.

Then I hear Alex. He's yelling like crazy, and he's right outside.

"What's going on?"

"They found meth in Alex's trailer," Ted says. "He's being escorted off the lot."

Mom explodes. "But we have a whole bunch of scenes to shoot. We'll get behind!"

"He's in violation," Sam explains. "You know the contract."

Mom has been real clear that if I get in trouble with drugs or alcohol, I'm fired. And it's the same for Alex.

"So . . . what do we do?" I ask.

"I'm writing Seth out. You're gonna have a new boyfriend."

What can I say, that I'm unhappy? Alex was poison, pure and simple.

Mom is like a statue. She must be thinking how easy it would be to write me out. It's scary. Of course, I'm the star, so they aren't going to do that. Only, that's not how she thinks. No matter how good things may be, Mom is always going to be clinging by her fingernails.

"I'll work over the weekend. We'll start shooting again on Monday," Ted says.

I doubt we're going to be shooting again any time soon. He can't possibly write Seth out that fast.

The funeral procession finally gets up and leaves us alone in the trailer. I can hear Alex's screams over the air-conditioning hum. On the other side of a scream like that is the black hole of being forgotten.

Mom says, "I need a drink." Then she laughs to herself. She sighs and says, "Small blessing. We can take off early. Let's get out of here, girl."

When we go out onto the lot, the California sun is painfully bright. A bright, hot desert where the sun burns away the lies.

CHAPTER 6

Flying on with the stars, with the clouds that love me,
flying in the dark when you cannot even see,
flying on forever . . . forever . . . forever . . .

What happened, what happened, what happened?

They were screaming down there, screaming at each other, and Beresford was frantic, hiding in the crawl space above his new hatch. Something awful had happened. He strained to hear, but they were talking so fast and saying so much he didn't understand. He was sure of only one thing: the fight was over *Swingles*.

When Beresford finished his hatch, the first thing he'd done was to go down into the apartment. He'd walked through the rooms, touching nothing. Trembling so hard he could barely control himself, he'd gone from room to room. He'd touched Melody's blue silk bedspread and watched the sun go down through her huge window.

When he'd heard them yelling as they came down the outside hall, he'd levered himself back up into the crawl space and pulled his hatch closed.

As he listened, they came into the living room and Melody screamed, "He attacked me! What don't you get about that? He's a druggie and a potential rapist and he's *gone*, Mom. And it is NOT my fault!"

"Honey, I know it, and I hate it, but we might lose the show anyway. It's not your fault, but the network is embarrassed."

"The *network*? You're scaring me, Mom, you really are."

"We need the money, Mel!"

"You need it, not me. If I had my way, we'd still be in Calabasas."

"And you'd be flipping burgers and singing 'Memories' in the Calabasas school talent show."

Their voices drifted off. They'd gone to the kitchen.

Swingles was over?

Their voices rose again, and then glass broke. He clapped his hands over his ears. They were throwing things, and that could not be good.

He just ached to go down there and take her in his arms and somehow make it all better, but Frank, the new super, was hunting him like crazy, and if he got found, he didn't know what would happen. He couldn't get thrown out of the Beresford. This was home.

Melody's bedroom door slammed. He slid over to the crawl space above it and pressed his ear against the rough plaster of the ceiling.

Crying came up from below, long, bitter sobs.

Very carefully, he moved back off the ceiling and down into the chase between Melody's room and the stairwell. From here, he could stay near her, and somehow maybe his love and his hope for her would help her.

He settled in, trying to get comfortable. He would guard her all night. Later, he'd sleep in his own tiny space on the roof, but not until after he was sure she was okay. It was real tight in here, and he had to keep twisting and turning so his legs wouldn't go to sleep. If he was very still, he could hear her breathing.

Instead of the sounds of sleep, he heard a shuffling noise. Then the wallboard seemed to shift a little.

"Get out of my wall, you creep!" Then *bang*, right in his face, and *bang bang bang*! "I know you're in there, you sicko, and I'm gonna call the cops and get you put away!"

He was frozen with fear. She *knows*, and she *hates me*.

His heart broke as he quickly reached over to the crawl space that crossed 5052, then hurried along the beams. He headed for the elevator shaft, oblivious to the tears that were blinding him.

This was the top floor, so the way to the roof for him was to climb the cables into the elevator room, then go out through the service door. He never, ever used the stairs. He understood cameras very well, and he didn't want to be seen on any of the security system screens in the basement.

He rushed out onto the roof and ran. He ran all the way to the far end, then around the edges. He got up on the rail and ran the rail, crying out and waving his arms, trying to make the feelings of sorrow and upset leave him.

He ran swiftly, deftly, and when he came to the spot where Daddy had fallen, he stopped. As he always did, he looked down into the alley. At night it was lit only by the one light over the side door. He looked down, and as always, he called out, cupping his hands around his mouth and shouting with all his might, "Daddy! Daddy!" Then he went on—or, he was about to go on—when he saw something below.

What he saw was a face like the face he'd seen peering at him the day Daddy was pushed, the same glittering lenses, the same robot appearance. Somebody was using a set of night-vision goggles to look up the side of the building.

That would be Frank or one of the other workers. They would be looking for him.

Had Melody told them? Were the police coming?

He shrank back from the edge and moved toward his tiny space on top of the elevator control shack, a tool storage shed just four feet high and nine long that had not been pulled off after construction was completed.

As he climbed the side of the shack, he saw one of the doors to the roof slowly open. For an instant, he was transfixed. Disbelieving. He quickly jumped down and in three strides concealed himself behind the shack, back where the water towers hissed and the bats lived.

A figure came out into the middle of the roof and stood. It was all in white, a woman, her back to him. The wind blew the thin white gown around her.

Then she turned a little, and a shock as powerful as lightning went through him. It was Melody.

She walked straight ahead, going toward the edge that dropped down to the building's marquee and front entrance. As she got closer to the edge, she walked faster. And now she spread her arms out and let the wind blow her white gown back, and he saw her body in its perfection outlined against the glow of the city. He knew that she was perfect and of the high world, and he was not perfect, hardly a person at all.

Her voice rose, magic in the night. She was singing a song he'd heard her working on.

"So not free, so not free, when will you come and take me?

So not free, so not free, where is the love I need? So not free, so not free . . ."

She bent over and the words went away, and she was sobbing into her hands.

He wanted to help her so much that he actually reached out and took a few steps toward her.

She straightened up and went even closer to the edge. She was right against the railing now, and he was thinking that she must not get up on it, that she was not like him; she didn't know how to climb and balance. She raised a leg, and he almost moaned aloud.

Then she leaned forward. If she went just a few more inches, she was going to topple over the edge.

She held her hands to her head and uttered the saddest cry he'd ever heard in his life.

She bent forward further. Her thighs were tight against the rail.

No!

She stood very still now, her hands at her sides as she looked to where the moon hung low. Every inch of his body and every whisper of his soul made him want to run to her and put his arms around her fragile waist and draw her back from the edge. But if he surprised her, she would lose her footing.

Now she sang again, her voice climbing the tower of the

air, pealing through the wind as if there was no wind. "So not free, so not free, please come for me, please come for me. Unlock the perfect prison of my life, make me new, make me true, 'cause I'm so not free, so not free."

The words moved him to his core, and he felt their meaning, the eternal sense of loss that is at the center of every human heart, and he thought they were the truest words he had ever known, a cry to the night and the moon to come and unlock the prison of life.

Again she swayed, and once again she raised her arms. He could see her naked form in the thin robe, outlined by the moonlight.

He thought if he ran fast enough, he could maybe grab her from behind and pull her back, then throw himself to one side among the air-conditioning equipment to her left. Once he was up under there, he would somehow make his way to the other side of the roof, where there was more than one place to slip away into the building and be gone.

Sure, but what if he missed? Or was too slow? If she heard him coming? It was just too dangerous to even try.

He stepped back into the shadows of the elevator shack and cried out as loud as he could, "So not free, so not free!"

She froze. It looked as if she was riveted to the rail.

He bit his tongue almost to bleeding, then covered his mouth with his hands. He stood as still as a statue.

Suddenly she whirled around. Her eyes were glaring, her lips twisted with pure hate—it was like the face of some kind of beautiful monster—and her hands were out in front of her like claws.

"I hate you," she said, venom in her words. Then her eyes widened and she screamed, "I HATE YOU, I HATE YOU, I HATE YOU!"

He smashed his hands against his ears and cried out as if he was being struck, because that's how it felt.

She was looking right at him. Did she see him? The light was behind her, but it wasn't very bright, so he couldn't be sure.

With a single broad step, he slipped behind a cooler tower. Now peering through the falling water, he watched her as she turned once again toward the edge.

For another long moment, she leaned out over the abyss.

Then she straightened up. Turned around. Without looking again in his direction, without making a sound, she strode to the stairway door.

Then she was gone, back into the building that was her home and, he now understood, her prison. He didn't know if she would actually have jumped, not even if she'd been planning to. But he feared it.

His heart went with her down the hard steel stairs to the luxury and torment of the fiftieth floor. In his mind was the image of her glowing in the moonlight, and another image, of her lying in the alley as his father had, arms spread, absolutely still.

He slid into his space and closed his eyes. He stayed there a while. He lay listening, determined to stay alert in case she came back. But his thoughts went to those night-vision goggles.

He got his rose and cradled it.

The rose of life and the rose of happiness, he thought, and in that moment he made a decision. It was dangerous, he knew, and it was foolish, and it would take from him the thing he loved the most. But he also knew that his rose could bring Melody happiness, too, and maybe even help her somehow.

He slipped into the electrical room through the hatch he'd made from his little space, then dropped down along the hot, humming cables and into the fiftieth-floor crawl space. There was rock music coming from 5052 and, from across the hall, a man and a woman arguing. Apartment 5050 was silent. He went out across the ceiling of the den and did something he never did when somebody was home.

He put his hand on his hatch. Closed his fingers around the little latch he'd screwed into it and opened it.

Silence below. Darkness. A faint odor of something sweet—perfume, he thought.

He dropped down into the closet. Hardly breathing, he listened for movement in the room beyond.

Not a sound.

He stepped into the hallway, then stopped listening.

All he could hear was his own thrashing heart.

Why was he doing this? Was he crazy? But he had to. He wanted to give her the rose.

He stood before her door, pressed his ear against it, listened, and heard nothing from inside. Was she asleep?

Turning the handle carefully, he opened the door a crack. He waited. No sound. He opened it further. Her bed was a dark pool, her form on it a curled shadow.

In three long, silent steps, he was beside her. He looked down at her face, shadowy and gorgeous, the full lips held in a line that suggested great sadness.

Trembling, he laid a hand on her broad forehead, feeling fear and electric pleasure as he touched her for the first time. For a moment he was paralyzed, unable to break the connection.

Then he took his rose from his pocket and placed it on the pillow beside her face.

He stepped quickly out of the room and slipped ghostlike down the hall and through the den, drawing himself into the crawl space and closing his hatch behind him.

He slipped into the darkness and hidden passages of the building, leaving behind, like a sacrifice and a talisman, the most precious thing he possessed.

CHAPTER 7

Frank waited miserably in Mr. Szatson's big office in his magnificent home. He wasn't precisely sure why he'd been called to come here, but it couldn't be good, that was certain.

He stared out through the glass wall toward the beautiful swimming pool. A woman sat beside it under an umbrella, reading a book in the sun and listening to music that was too faint to make out.

"My wife," Szatson said sarcastically as he came hurrying into the room. He threw his athletic form down behind the huge desk and fixed his dark, quick eyes on Frank.

Frank knew perfectly well that Mr. Szatson had hired him to do fires. So, probably that's what this meeting was about. Some Szatson development somewhere was being stalled by some jerk refusing to move, and he needed to be burned out.

Szatson looked at him for so long that it became uncomfortable, and Frank had to look away. It was an intimidation technique, he supposed. If so, it wasn't going to work. He was going to need more than his pitiful super's salary to do a fire.

"What's our present vacancy status?"

Frank blinked with surprise. He wasn't often wrong about people, but this was not the question he had expected. "I've seen a steady stream of move-outs, sir."

"What's the complaint log look like?"

"Not a lot. The rents need to come down—that's our problem."

"Frank, I want to tell you something. The move-outs don't matter."

That made no sense, but he was the boss. "Uh, okay."

"In fact, I want you to encourage more of them. Hassle people a little. Nothing illegal, of course, don't go that far. But you can cut back air-conditioning, drop hot water pressure. You can do that sort of thing."

"Sure, but why?"

Again, Luther Szatson's eyes met his. "Frank, Frank, Frank." He chuckled. "Have you learned the building?"

"Absolutely."

"Then you know how it all works, the power systems, the air, the steam, all of that?"

"Yes, sir."

"And how much fuel oil does it carry, Frank, at any given time?"

Frank was so astonished that he almost couldn't reply, because that question told him instantly where this was going. But no—*no*. The Beresford was too big. It was—oh, God, it would be the fire of the century. He swallowed hard and fought to gather enough spit to talk. "We generally have about twenty thousand gallons on hand. More in the winter. The capacity is thirty thousand gallons."

"And where is that?"

"Where is the fuel oil stored?"

"Exactly."

"In the storage tanks. There are three of them under the machinery floor." Szatson must be quizzing him to make sure he knew his stuff. Okay, he'd pass this quiz.

"And where is the elevator shaft in relation to this storage area?"

"Uh, the shafts come down—the service cars bottom on the tank floor."

"The elevator shaft is actually open all the way from the top of the building to the bottom, isn't it?"

"Well, yeah, of course."

"That would be a major violation, Frank."

"Yeah, but the doors down there are code doors. Fire doors. So any problem is gonna be contained, if that's what you're worried about, Mr. Szatson."

Szatson's eyes smiled, but his words were spat right in Frank's face. "It's none of your business what I'm worried about."

Frank would sooner have been watched by a cobra. He needed some kind of clarification. Because if Mr. Szatson was going to torch a fifty-story apartment building full of people, Frank was not his man. No way.

"You're saying I need to do everything I can to increase vacancies, Mr. Szatson? Because I'm not quite sure, here."

"Let me ask you this. If something happened in the basement, if there was a fuel fire, how well protected are we?"

The words hung in the air. People would be killed. With his record, the cops would be all over him. If he got convicted, he'd get the needle.

"Frank, are we protected? Or do I need to do something about that shaft?"

"Well, those fire doors would close. If it was a straight flamer, no problem. The sprinklers would take care of it before the fire department even got there. The thing is, though, if the fuel tanks went up, they'd blow the doors off, and then you'd see that shaft work like a chimney. You'd have fire all the way to the top of the structure in a matter of seconds."

Then he thought an incredible, chilling thought: Was this *why* the elevator shaft went down to the fuel storage tanks? Had Szatson always planned to torch the Beresford?

But why hadn't the insurance company seen it? One reason and one only: Mr. Szatson was in the insurance business, too. You could be sure, though, when the Beresford burned, it wouldn't be his money that would come out of the insurance trust to pay the gigantic claim. No, that would be the money of innocent investors.

How much would he collect? Easily half a billion dollars and probably more. There would be lawsuits galore, of course, from the survivors and the families of the dead—for there would be many dead—but the suits would also be covered by liability insurance.

Instead of making a small monthly profit on the Beresford, Szatson was going to cash out in what was bound to be one of the most spectacular fires in Los Angeles history.

"Is it doable?" Szatson asked. His voice was very quiet. "I mean, could it happen? A fire like that?"

"I don't think those fuel tanks are that dangerous. That oil takes special treatment to burn—that's why you've got blowers on the fireboxes."

"Well, good. Then I'm not gonna lose any sleep over it." He went to a drawer and removed a file. "I got a variance from the city for that shaft. They let me off the hook, thank God. It was an honest mistake."

Frank knew that he had to have paid plenty for that variance. No honest inspector would let a violation that dangerous go unrepaired.

"So, Frank, are we together on this?"

Frank knew he was the best torch in the game, and Luther Szatson had reached out for him.

He took a deep breath and spoke. "I want you to know that I understand very clearly, Mr. Szatson." He would not say that he would do it, though. He would not do it. First, it was too dangerous. Second, he'd never killed anyone. He did arson, not murder.

Szatson strolled to the glass wall that overlooked the pool.

Frank interpreted this as a signal that the meeting was over and started to get up.

"No, no," Szatson said, "we're not quite finished here." He opened the folder on his desk. "I'm looking at a complaint here."

"About me? From a tenant?"

"It's from a tenant's lawyer. The singer on fifty."

"Yeah?"

"The thing is, this lawyer is claiming that somebody is bothering the girl. Somebody is—listen to this—'utilizing shaftways and crawl spaces to stalk Miss McGrath.'"

That damn squatter. Frank held up his hand. "Say no more. It's taken care of."

"Wylie said that. Christopher before him. Now you say it."

"Except I can do it."

Szatson glared. "Then why haven't you?" His voice was acid. Frank knew this shadow man could turn out to be a witness, and witnesses were dangerous.

"I've confirmed that he's there. That's a start."

"I don't need a start, I need a finish!"

"He's good at what he does."

"Get the job done!"

"I'll take care of him."

"If this bastard uses the chases, fine. He can fall."

Frank knew exactly what those words meant. His boss had just told him to kill the squatter.

"Yes, sir," he agreed, "he can fall. But then we have a police investigation inside the building."

"He falls, he disappears."

Frank could smell the stink of fear in the room, the sharp odor of his own sweat.

"Well," Szatson said, "I think we've reached an understanding. Am I right?"

Frank had just been asked to set a fire that was certain to kill and to murder a squatter. He temporarily froze.

"Frank, you know why you came out of the house early? Why you're off the parole list?"

"I've got an idea."

"It's the right idea. I did it, and I can undo it. I can make it look like you forged the release documents. *You*, Frank. You'll go back in."

And, as Frank knew all too well, this time it would be for good.

So he was being given a choice: kill people and risk being executed, or refuse to do it and spend the rest of his life in prison, convicted of using forged documents to escape.

He sucked breath. Life in prison for certain against the possibility of a death sentence. A certainty against a possibility.

He made his choice.

"You're gonna get your work done, sir. Just like you want it done."

Szatson smiled. Somehow the brightness of his teeth made the deal even more terrifying.

Back in his car, Frank sat for a long time. "So what happens to me?" he muttered into the silence. "What happens to me then?"

The answer was, Szatson went on down the road amassing his billions, and a little guy like Frank—well, maybe he got something, and maybe he didn't.

As he angled his car down into the city streets, he felt the tightness of frustration constricting his throat. Stopping at a light on Franklin, he watched a bunch of kids from Hollywood High School cross the street and head toward Starbucks.

When the light changed, he found that his foot had been pressing the brake so hard that it had cramped in the arch.

He drove on back to the Beresford with one thought in mind: the creep who was using the shafts was about to find out that when you got an unexpected push, the fall was long and the landing hard.

CHAPTER 8

We're in the middle of a media frenzy, and I'm totally thrown, I have to say. It's over Alex, of course. I should have expected it, but I didn't. I woke up this morning thinking only about the creep on the roof, then Lupe, who cleans our place, called to say the doorman wouldn't let her in because he thought she was with the reporters.

Now I'm gonna have to do a papi walk just to get out of the building. It makes me wish I could fly, and suddenly a new song is in my mind, "Flying on Forever." Every kid in the world will understand this song, I know it.

I'm still thinking about the unbelievable fight we had. The worst ever, I think.

We meet in the front hall, and the first words out of Mom's mouth are, "You look *wonderful*." She's trying to make up, but I still can't.

Now the doorbell rings, and Julius is here. The super, Frank, is with him.

"We're ready to move," Julius says, and Frank goes, "I've got the back entrance open, and we have security in the lobby to make it look like you're about to come through."

"We want to go through the lobby," Mom says.

"*Mom!*" But she's right. Of course we do.

So I stand in silence as the elevator goes down.

Frank says, "Mrs. McGrath, we have that other situation under control."

"Thank you."

I would never tell Mom that I saw him on the roof last night, because she would go totally *insane* if she knew I'd been up there. She'd put armed guards in the stairwell.

I don't think I wanted to jump. I don't know. Maybe what I wanted was to fly.

The doors open—and there, in the middle of the hungry crowd, the first thing I see is the grinning face of this tiny woman with huge glasses who says, "Melody, I'm Amber. From *People*?"

Then a papi I don't know says, "Melody, is it true you do meth, too? That the cops are covering for you?"

"Amber," Mom says, taking her by the arm as we go through the camera clickathon, "you were supposed to call!"

We're an entourage now, me and Mom and Julius and Frank and Amber. Not a big entourage, maybe, but enough to make me appear to be the star.

Shouted question: "Melody, is *Swingles* totally dead?"

"Nothing is ever totally dead," Mom yells back.

"How do you feel about Alex going to jail?"

For a second, I'm thrown. What is this about *jail*?

"Did he rape you, Melody?"

Then we are outside under the marquee and the limo is there. Thank God.

The limo smells like bacon, and I discover that we have a nice breakfast waiting—scrambled eggs and coffee and bacon. I want to love Mom again.

I'm not even chewing a mouthful of food yet when Mom says, "Walker is on guitar, and Mickey is on drums again. So what do you have for them, sweetie?"

Mom is 1,000 percent business, as always.

"I have 'So Long, Boyfriend' and 'Love Without You' and two new ones."

"Okay." She puts out her hand.

"Um, actually, they're in my head."

"You do understand that studio time burns fifteen hundred dollars an hour?"

"They're in my head!"

"They need to be on paper!"

"When I'm in the iso booth, I'll do them. You can work with the arranger. We'll put it together as we go."

"So, basically, we have just the two songs. And that's it."

"Mom, we have four songs and probably more, and you have to respect my process! They *will* come out." I get so mad I just boil over, and right in front of the damn *People* lady, too.

"And who scores? Who turns this crap into music?"

"Whoever you hired to turn this crap into music!"

I catch on that she *wants* the *People* lady to write awful things about her. She wants to be known as a harridan, a slave driver, because it makes a lot better copy than if she was wonderful and smart and sweet.

I eat my breakfast and watch her and think about her. This is the woman who came sneaking into my room last night and put her hand on my forehead, then proceeded to leave a weathered old silk rose on my pillow as some kind of odd peace offering. It looks like something off a garbage truck. And now I'm going to conduct an experiment.

I take the rose from my purse. "By the way, Mom, thanks for this."

She looks at it. In the jump seats Julius and Amber gobble more eggs. But Amber is not oblivious. She is doing her reporter thing of disappearing into the woodwork so, hopefully, she can pile dirt on me. As she gobbles, she watches.

Mom looks at it. "What's this supposed to mean?"

Which is not the reaction I expected. "Um, maybe that's my question."

She picks it up. "This is filthy." She rolls down the window and tosses it out.

Suddenly I want to scream because I know what it is. It's from *him*. He saw me on the roof and he stopped me. Maybe I didn't need to be stopped, but now I know *he can get into our apartment*.

My breakfast comes up all over everything and everybody, and I am horribly embarrassed and totally sick.

"Oh, Lord, honey."

"You want me to stop, ma'am?"

"No, Louie, we're fine, don't stop, for God's sake!"

I'm fighting for control, but my body is suddenly not my own. I remember him standing there in the shadows on the roof, and another heave comes.

Julius gets his arms around me and helps me back into the seat while Mom finds paper towels somewhere under the bar and wipes up. Then she produces a new shirt, which I change into.

"I have to get out—I'm going to be sick," Amber yells.

"Open the windows for her, but *do not stop*."

So we go on down the Ten with the windows open and traffic all around us and the papis frantically trying to get up beside us so they can get a shot of whatever in hell is happening in here.

We're going to Reynolds, one of the most legendary recording studios in the world, which I like because it has a real private feeling once you are inside. Plus, the isolation booths are big and comfy, and if I'm going to spend my whole day in one, what I don't need is claustrophobia.

"Okay, honey, okay now, it's gonna be good. It's gonna be good. Am I riding you too hard?"

She is cleaning me up, fixing my face, her eyes full of pride and love.

"Mom, I'm so sorry."

"We're fine. We're going to have an extraordinary day."

I feel the car stop and whisper to Mom, "I'm not scared." Mom's look has love in it, but also a sharpness that *does* scare me.

The papis are parking on the sidewalk and running toward us.

"Now just look out the window, don't say anything, and let them shoot you."

So I sit amid the machine gun clicking of the cameras, which is amazingly intense. I smile, and, yes, there is this thrill that goes through me when I realize that they are working in relays because there are so many of them.

When the window goes up, they are all gone. I sit back and close my eyes, and for just a second the world is not there. Then I hear the gargling sound of Mom sucking her plastic cigarette. I open my eyes and watch Amber writing on a pad.

I mean, she actually does this. Every other reporter I've met never wrote a thing down and just made up all my quotes. This is real, though. It's not a tab, it's *People*, for Chrissake.

The door opens, and we're in the forecourt, which is full of bamboo and palm trees and blooming lantana. Then Willie comes out with Sassy Lester, my arranger.

"Mel, they're just brilliant, *brilliant*," she says. She looks at Mom. "Oh my God, Hilda, aren't they *fabulous*?"

"I know. We're so proud of her."

I actually haven't played any of these demos for Mom yet. And for a reason—she'll be too critical.

We go down the long hall paneled with blond wood and hung with pictures of people from ancient history, like Sandra Dee, and more recent ones, like Sister Hazel. There is a picture of me at the end of the hall, the one that was taken by Rod Gilliard last April. 'Course I know that it will be gone eventually, replaced by a picture of the next instant superstar.

But it sure does make me feel important, especially when I go into the isolation booth where I will spend the next however many hours. Inside I find the spritzer of mint Listerine that I like, a box of Altoids, and six-packs of Evian and fruit punch Gatorade. Nobody asked me my preferences. They found out on their own.

My demo comes through, and the first song we run is "Flying on Forever," which is almost whispered, with long bass notes backing it up, and I'm thinking we should add something like a theremin when Sassy says into my earphones, "When I heard this, I said to Willie, this is slow and dreamy."

"Kids need to be able to dance to it," I say. "Think slow dancing, just a few kids in somebody's rec room with all the lights turned off," I add.

"I think our girl's done this before," Willie says.

Then my voice comes into my ears, and I start singing to it, and I feel like I'm flying.

"Flying on with the stars, with the clouds that love me, flying in the dark when you cannot even see, flying on forever...forever...forever..." Again I'm up on that railing and the wind is blowing my silk nightgown, and I sing, "When you are remembered, you're not remembered at all, nobody's real, nobody falls, nobody at all...'cause we're all flying on forever...forever...forever."

I stop and after a second the scratch track stops too. Willie says, "Good. We'll take some of those."

"I need a punch in 'you're not remembered,'" I say. "I dropped off-key."

Then Mom's voice comes into the mix. "Is this a song about suicide?"

"No, Mom, it's about flying."

"We don't need people blaming us for kids killing themselves, Mel."

"My music is about coping with emotions, not giving in to them."

I remember the weirdo standing back in the shadows. Somehow he had stopped me.

"Flying on forever," I sing, "forever . . . forever . . . forever," and so it goes, on and on. I do my lyrics again and again and again. Hopefully what comes out the other end will sound rad, and I'll get amazing downloads and have a hit.

Some musicians will do fifty takes or more. But I can't do it that way. I'll sing it through five or six times, feeling it down deep in my blood.

Then we move on to "So Not Free," which I think will be the big seller on this album. I can see Mom outside the sound room with her plastic cigarette, glaring. She is not liking these songs.

"You think you're on the road, you think you're gonna go, but you're so not free, so not free . . . so not free . . . so not free. . . . You think there are no bars, but they put them around your heart. . . . You're so not free, so not free. . . ."

"NO, NO, NO!" Mom throws up her arms. "This is all crazy. This isn't music. There's hardly any rhyme—it's almost unsing-able! It's dark, depressive crap, and I won't have it!"

"I think it sounds great, Sassy. Let's do it again. I'm ready," I say.

"I believe we're in mid-freakout here," Willie says under

his breath. "Mrs. McGrath, we were going to do that take again. Are you all right?"

"Okay, fine, do it again, but you will NOT get paid. None of you! Money tap is closed." Her eyes pop practically out of her head and she looks at me. "And I *can* do it. Legally, I have the right, *little girl!*"

So I pull off my headset and go out into the observation room, where Mom paces and Amber sits scribbling wildly.

Time for me to take over. "Mother, I would appreciate it if you could go out and get Louie to take you home."

"I'm getting in that car, all right, but so are you, you self-obsessed, self-destructive little bitch. And you're gonna go to a goddamn shrink and get some antidepressants."

"Well, that's very insightful of you. Do you know that I went up on the roof last night, and I almost went over? And do you also know that it was *not you* who made me go up there and lean against that rail, and it was *not you* who made me come down?"

She grabs me and *shakes, shakes, shakes* until my eyes and neck hurt, and finally Amber says, "Hey there, hey there," and grabs Mom's shoulder.

"This is between me and her, dammit!" Mom lunges at Amber. "Gimme that notebook!" She grabs it and rips out pages and stuffs them in her mouth. "Your lies taste like paper," she says as the pages come flying out.

Amber sort of recovers herself but looks absolutely horrified.

Then Sassy is there, standing in the doorway. Sassy is maybe thirty. She sings in cabarets of the kind Mom likes, so they have some sort of bond. Sassy has a sailor cut, and she's real thin. Today she has on a Three Wolves T-shirt and jeans at least as old as me.

"It's all brilliant, you know."

"But it's not gonna SELL," my mom says. "Kids like—" She dances a kind of crazed little jig. "They like to dance and laugh and love! Like I did! It hasn't changed. It'll never change."

Silence. Everybody is now in the room with us, and every single person disagrees with Mom. You can hear it in the total vacuum.

"It'll never change!"

She throws herself down on the couch and jams her headphones back on. She takes out her plastic cigarette and throws it across the room. She lights a Marlboro, takes a long drag, dragons the smoke out her nose, and says, "Okay, so Mommy's being bad again. Call a cop!"

I won that one. We go on with the session, and I find a rhythm, grabbing songs out of some kind of spirit wind that is blowing through my head. I know we're just laying down scratch tracks at this point, but they'll lead to something. Anyway, we end the day with five finished songs, "So Not

Free," "Flying on Forever," "Blue Roses," "Love Without You," and, of course, "So Long, Boyfriend."

As we're heading back to the car, Mom apologizes to Amber.

Amber says nothing. I can't even begin to imagine what's going to appear in *People*, but it won't be pretty.

Mom is still smoking, so I crack a window.

She reaches over, closes it.

"Mom, I can't stand—"

"I put up with your crap."

"I can't stand us fighting! Why are we fighting? Why can't we stop?"

"Why are we fighting? Because you're sixteen years old and I'm the dumbest mom who ever existed."

"I hope I'm not that much of a cliché."

She reaches over and pats my knee. And, in this way, a truce is declared. She says to Louie, "We go in on Tischer Court. The super's got the back open for us." Then to me, "The party's over for the papis."

"Thank you, Mom."

Frank is there—he comes out the door as we pull up. He looks huge, like a guard coming out of a guardhouse. He must be six four. I imagine him carrying me upstairs.

There's an elevator waiting at the end of the long gray hall near the security office. In the office I see all the screens, all the images from the security cameras on every floor, and

I wonder if Frank knows who the stalker is. But I don't want to ask him. I don't want to say anything because there will just be more hell over it with Mom. If Mom knew he'd been in the apartment, there would be no peace.

We arrive at our floor.

"Thanks, Frank," Mom says, and I hear in her voice the certain tone that she reserves for men she likes, a sort of smoothness with a whisper of bedtime in it. But he's at least ten years younger than she is.

As we enter the foyer, I see an arrangement on the big table, a beautiful spray of flowers.

"Hi there, Mel. Hi, Hilda."

A man comes strolling out of the living room, and at first I think it's some new beau who has been given the run of the apartment without even a mention to me, but then I am introduced.

"Melody, this is Dr. Singer."

Somehow, she has managed to call a shrink and get him over here.

I head straight for the door.

"Mel!"

"No, Mom, I'm not staying. If you want me to see a doctor, ask me. Don't ambush me."

"You're a minor."

"I'm a human being, and I have human rights!"

"You're a child, and you're in trouble, and you need help."

She turns away, strides toward the wall of windows. "Oh, God," she murmurs, "help me."

I realize that she is absolutely terrified for me.

I look toward the front door and want so badly to just walk through it and keep going forever, just like in my song.

Except, except, *except*, I do want my career. It's not the fame that matters—it's the kind of musical inspiration that happened today.

"Okay," I say to Dr. Singer. "What are we doing?"

"I'm here because your mother is concerned."

I look at her. She looks right back. The defiance there makes me mad. The terror makes me sad. She says, "Honey, please."

So I go into the den and drop down on the couch. "Is this how you want me?"

"Melody, I want you to be comfortable. I just want us to get to know each other today. We'll keep talking. But I want to put something right on the table now. Do you know what a suicide intervention is?"

Ohmygod. This guy must be from a suicide watch.

I say nothing.

"So tell me, did you do what your mom says you did? What you told her?"

I just had the best day of my whole life, and the worst day of my whole life.

"I don't know what I said."

He takes out a pocket recorder. He presses a button and I

hear *me*: "Do you know that I went up on the roof last night, and I almost went over?"

He stops it. "That is you?"

My throat closes. I want to talk, but I can't. I want to shake my head *no no no*, but I can't.

"And you spent the whole day recording songs that can't be used. Suicide songs?"

"This is totally insane. Because this was the best day I've ever had. I mean, songs I didn't even know I had in me came out, and my arranger—who is the one who actually knows, not Mom—she says they're brilliant."

"She's a paid employee. Of course she's enthusiastic. But this material needs to disappear."

Could Mom actually have my songs *erased*? Would she?

"Where is my music?"

"Excuse me?"

"You know what I said, you bastard. WHERE IS MY MUSIC?" I jump up. "MOM! MOM!"

She's in the living room, smoking and drinking vodka.

I approach her. "Did you erase my day?"

"Darling, you can't go out there with that stuff. It's horrible. *Horrible!*"

And then I am on her. I am hitting her, slamming her, kicking her, and I feel myself almost immediately being pulled off, and I scream—boy, do I scream. I scream with all my might for help, for anyone to come, for *him* to come because whoever he is, he's going to be better than the living hell this place has become.

I'm dragged across the room by this prick, who is stronger than he looks.

I go limp. What's the use?

"Melody, we're going to give you a little sedative," I hear him say.

Mom nods.

"That was probably the best session at Reynolds in *history*!"

"When you wake up in the morning," Mom says, "there will be a composer here, and tomorrow the three of us are going to start creating some music that people want to hear."

He takes my arm.

"Don't you dare touch me!"

Then there is a pain in my shoulder and I jerk away, but it's too late.

Already the world is going. I can feel the covers coming up around me.

I see the sunset out my window, red at the horizon, gold higher up.

Then it is dark.

CHAPTER 9

Beresford had never felt anything like this before in his life.

All day he had stayed in Melody's apartment, forcing himself not to open her drawers or her closet, looking instead in the fridge at the things she ate and drank, the diet sodas, the cheese and roasted chicken, the cold cuts, the mint ice cream. He would take a taste and close his eyes and let the flavors fill his head and think, "*She* has tasted this taste; *she* knows this flavor."

Only when their maid had come in and cleaned had he hidden, and then just to go up his hatch and linger there, waiting for the vacuum cleaner to stop and the singing to fade away, which it did, as always, in a couple of hours.

He had looked for his rose, but it was not there, so that meant she liked it and had it with her. Good.

Usually, they were home late, so he wasn't expecting the man who came when the sun was midway down the western sky. Still, it was easy to slip into the den and back up into the crawl space. He'd lain along one of the beams, listening. The man went into Melody's room and searched it carefully. He could hear him turning pages, and he wondered if Melody kept a notebook. Why not? She could probably write and read and all that.

When they came home, the man met them and there was yelling that made Beresford stuff his fist in his mouth so he wouldn't shout out his own rage at whatever they were doing to her. They were breaking her heart and maybe even hurting her. He could hear the terror and the sorrow in her voice.

Then the man put her to sleep. He'd heard that, too, had heard her scream and beg for him not to, and then her voice went low, and the man—a doctor—said she would sleep until morning.

Beresford sweated out the minutes until the place was quiet. He was going to enter an occupied apartment again. He hadn't been able to stop himself last night, and he couldn't now.

Slowly, carefully, he opened his hatch and looked down into the den closet. All was quiet. No light shone under the door. So he slipped down to the floor, then carefully slid the door open a crack.

The den was full of shadows.

Moving quickly and silently, he stepped out of the closet and crossed the room. There was light shining under this door, but none of the shadows revealed movement. Also, not a sound. Carefully, he grasped the doorknob and turned it.

The hall was dimly lit by a lamp in the living room. Melody's mom sat on the couch reading papers of some sort. She listened to soft music.

Beresford needed to be with Melody.

He slid silently along the wall to her door, then touched the doorknob as if it was a delicate blossom and gently turned it.

He was in. The curtains were drawn. With three quick steps he crossed to her bedside. He could just see her in the darkness, her face glowing as if with an inner light.

He bent closer, cupping his hands around her cheeks, not daring to touch her. He could feel her warmth and smell a faint perfume. She was so wonderful. Just so very wonderful. He drank her in with his eyes, touched the faint heat that lingered around her head, and longed for something he didn't understand and couldn't name but that made his whole body ache.

Finally, he sat on the floor beside the bed. At once shaking with fear and thrilled beyond words, he leaned his head against the mattress. He could feel the faint tickle of her breath against his cheek.

Hesitant, hardly daring, he slid his hand up until it just touched her arm.

After a time, she sighed and shifted in the bed. When she stopped, he was already halfway across the room.

Now she lay with a hand dangling off the edge of the bed. He crept back.

Her face was now turned toward the wall. His heart hammering, his breath shallow and quick, he knelt beside the bed, bent forward, and kissed her cheek.

Her skin smelled of flowers. His face close to hers, he imagined that he could send her his thoughts: "I love you with all my heart, Melody McGrath, and I give myself to you forever."

Her sleep continued on, undisturbed.

He did not kiss her again, but he also did not leave.

Sometime very late, he heard voices. It was the doctor and Melody's mom.

There was no time to do anything except slide under the bed. A bare second later, four feet entered the room.

"See, she's peaceful," the doctor said. "It's not the Nitraze-pam anymore. It's just natural sleep. She'll wake up normally and feel a lot better."

"I don't know if she hates me or what."

"Sixteen is very conflicted."

"You can say that again."

Beresford was furious. This man was supposed to be a doctor, and he sounded like one, but he shouldn't be in the apartment this late with the patient's mother. That was not right.

"What am I gonna do with her?"

"Make money, Hilda. You have two years before you lose control of her."

"I've got her album back on the charts. I've got her show sold out."

"And she's ever so grateful."

"Hardly."

In reply, he chuckled. Then the feet came together and Beresford's face burned, because he heard the sound of kissing.

Finally he saw them walking out, her arm around his waist. When they were gone, he pulled himself out from under the bed—but as he did so, he heard something else.

Listening, he froze. It was in the ceiling, a faint creaking.

But there was a lot of wind tonight, so maybe it was the building. Nobody but him ever went in the crawl spaces.

He resumed his vigil beside his sleeping beauty, wanting to protect her but not sure exactly how to go about it.

As before, she breathed softly, her breath warm on his cheek when he leaned near her.

He was just settling back down beside her bed when there was a sharp intake of breath. Before he could react, she shot up to a sitting position and her eyes opened wide. She was going to scream.

He laid his mouth beside her ear and whispered, "Don't scream, don't scream, please, please, please." In response there was a choked groan, then another. "Please, please, please . . ."

Then, for the first time in the world, the girl he loved spoke to him. She said in whispered breath, "Who are you?"

He raised his head and looked into the most perfect face he had ever known. His heart hammered and sweat came all over his shivering body, and he told her the truth. "I don't remember."

A frown flickered in her eyes, then her lips opened slightly and her eyes glanced away. "W-what?"

He thought she must be at the edge of total panic.

"I guess I had a name a long time ago, but I forgot it because no one talks to me."

He had never in his life wanted to hug somebody as much as he wanted to hug Melody. Impulsively, he kissed the end of her nose.

She smiled a little, but then wagged her finger in front of his face.

"How do you get in my room?"

"I live here."

"In my apartment? You *live* here?"

He pointed to the ceiling. "In there. All over. I live in the Beresford."

She looked at him a long time, her eyes rich with questions, her soft lips alternately touched with a smile, then trembling at the edge of fear.

"You know you're wearing a woman's blouse."

It was a shirt he got out of the trash in an apartment, so he was not sure what this meant.

"Yes," he said carefully.

"Are you a TV?"

He was confused. Wasn't it obvious that he was a person?

"Do I look like a TV?"

"No, except the blouse."

He looked down at himself. "It's not a TV." He felt it. "It's cloth."

Surprise washed her face, sparkles came into her eyes.

"What is going on here?"

"Shh! Shh!"

She got out of bed, swept across the room, and locked the door. "Man, I need coffee. Can you make coffee appear, magic boy?"

"Yeah, but we better go to a vacationer."

Suddenly there was light! Instinct made him go for the closet, then terror swept through him like a rush of fire, because his hatch was not in there.

She stood by the door with her hand on the light switch. She was looking at him now with frank, wide eyes. She came toward him.

"Turn around," she said.

He turned slowly.

Now her head was down, her cheeks flushing a soft pink.

"You're beautiful," she said.

"You're beautiful."

"You need to get out of here."

"I want to stay."

She smiled at him, which caused him to think again of the meaning of the word *love*. This was love. That was what he felt.

"I want to stay because I love you."

She tossed her head and laughed a little in her throat, and the way that sounded made his body stir. He longed to hold her but knew from TV that if he did what he wanted, it would make her upset.

He said, "Can we hold hands?"

Silently, she came to him. She held out her hand. He took it. They stood face-to-face, hands clasped almost formally, and he thought there must be something else he should do, but he didn't know what it was.

"You kissed my cheek. That's why I woke up. I dreamed you were a prince. Are you?"

"I don't know."

"A beautiful boy with magical powers who wakes the sleeping beauty."

She raised her face to his and brushed her lips against his cheek.

It was fire that tickled. He shuddered.

Then she looked up at him, her eyes shining, her lips just parted. She took his chin, drew it down, and brought his lips to hers. An instant passed that was like eternity for him. But then she turned away.

"You have to go."

"I want to live here now."

"You haven't met my mother."

He did not say how well he knew her mother. He did not say how well he knew her life.

"If she found you, she would have you arrested."

He'd seen that on TV. "I didn't commit a crime."

"I'm still jailbait, you know. How old are you?"

"I'm as old as you are."

"You're sixteen?"

"Yeah, I think so."

She gave him a sideways glance. "Can you count to ten?"

"I can count to a hundred. I can read some stuff."

"Where do you go to school?"

"Uh . . . I don't remember."

"You don't. You really don't." She folded her arms and looked him up and down. "Do you live in an apartment? Where are your parents?"

"Mom died. Luther killed Dad."

"Luther? Who is Luther?"

"I don't know. I just never forgot his name. He pushed Dad off the roof."

"My God. Did the cops come? Did they arrest this guy?"

"I don't know."

"This happened—when? Today?"

He shook his head. It was so long ago now, it felt like it was at the bottom of a well. In the dark of the past. "I had to hide or Luther would get me, too. Luther would kill me."

"So you hid . . . where?"

He dared not tell about his place, not even her.

"In here."

"In my room? Luther killed your dad, and you hid here?"

"Wait, wait, I'm trying to tell you. It happened when I was little."

"But—*what*? Where do you come from, then, a foster home?"

"I come from here."

"I think you'd better leave now."

He didn't want to. He really, really didn't want to. "Please let me stay."

"If my mother found you in here—I don't even want to think about it. Do you have any identification?"

He threw his arms around her. "Don't go on the roof like that again. Don't ever!"

She leaned against him for a moment with her full weight, and it felt so good that he said in his mind, "Never stop, never stop." But then she did stop.

He grabbed her hands. "Promise me."

"You can't ask me that, because—you just can't!"

She turned away from him. He thought of the little birds that sometimes got into the crawl spaces of the upper floors. He tried to catch them, but he never could, and they died. They always died.

She said, "You have to leave now."

"I can't. I'm scared for you."

"Oh, Lord, now a lurker fan who lives in the walls. Where does it end?"

"If you come back up on the roof, I'll be there," he said.

"I have a balcony."

"I'll be there."

Her eyes widened and then sort of seemed to flash, and he decided that, whenever possible, he would be no more than ten feet away from her. He wanted to say "you have to live," but it sounded selfish, so he said nothing.

He put his hands on her shoulders and held her, and looked down into that perfect face. He knew there was a great sadness in her and realized that, at all costs, his primary mission was to save the woman he loved.

Unable to speak, he turned from her and went quickly out the door, into the hall, and back to the den. In a moment he was up in the crawl space and racing off down the equipment chase and into the depths of the building.

He did not see the light that followed him as he dropped down the chase, but it was there, and it carried his fate with it, a terrible fate that was thundering toward him with all the fury of an avalanche.

CHAPTER 10

Ohmygosh! Ohmygosh! Oh, he was beautiful, he was *beautiful*, he was gentle and amazing, and he lives in the walls. *He lives in the walls*!

I—I—I think I should be furious—at him for breaking into my house, at this stupid building for its rotten security. I think I should sue their asses. I think somebody should call the cops and get this kid into foster care. I think the Luther thing should be followed up . . . and I think I really, really want to see him again.

Where does he go, what does he do? Where *did* he go? He just suddenly walked out of the room, and I went out behind him and he was *gone*!

Is he a ghost, a *real* ghost? No, because he kissed me. It was like how a little boy kisses you, all sloppy and hard. He was clumsy and his heart was beating like a motor, but he's *huge*, way over six feet, and handsome, too, with hair that makes him look wild, and those big soulful eyes and rippling arm muscles. The way he held me, it was like he was some kind of master of dance. I just fell into his arms. He made me feel like a feather, an adored, beautiful feather. Then the kiss, and it was just darling—he had no idea what to do, he was just way out of his depth.

And what's with the blouse? What is *that*? He thought I was calling him an *actual* TV set, not a cross-dresser, because he must have no idea what that is.

I am laughing so hard I have to hold my face in the pillow until I practically smother, but then I just roll around in bed imagining him in here with me. He is really strong, and I know why—because he climbs around in this building like some kind of wonderful, beautiful phantom of the skyscraper.

His hair is a huge, blond wave that frames his face and hangs down behind him. You can see on the sides where he cuts it, but not very well. What does he use, pinking shears?

His face is an open window. His eyes are wide and blue-gray. He looks like everything surprises him. When I kissed him, he was so surprised that he almost collapsed.

He's rough but sweet, and the way he was forcing himself

to hold back just thrilled me and made me feel more wanted than I've ever felt before—

"Stop that preening and get dressed!"

"Oh, Jesus! Mom, you scared me!"

"You live for the mirror. It's a sickness."

"You don't want close-ups of my zits ending up online, do you?"

She sighs. Her hair is in curlers; her face is so bare of makeup that her complexion looks as if she's been drained by a vampire.

"Feeling okay, Mom? Because you look really pale."

"I didn't get much sleep."

"Worrying about me, of course. So, my fault," I say sarcastically.

"I'm glad you got some sleep, at least."

"I've been up since four. Your boyfriend's dope didn't work all that well, I guess."

"He's a doctor, Melody."

"A doctor who I'd bet spent the night with his patient's mother? I'd like to see his credentials."

I run to my bathroom and slam the door. I know I'm being hard on Mom, but she's being hard on me, too. I mean, erasing my entire day of work at Reynolds? I'm expected to just forget it, I suppose, like some two-year-old who has about a thirty-second memory span.

All I can think about is *him*. How did he end up in here? There was a murder and he hid, so he says. This Luther, he hid from him. Why did Luther kill his dad? Or is it all a fantasy? What if he actually *does* have an apartment, or is just a damn stalker who lives in the Valley and snuck in?

No. He's real. A wild child.

I turn on the shower and get in. It's blue marble with gold fixtures, just like I wanted.

I'm amazed all over again, and kind of shivering while I stand looking down at the water sluicing me and think, what would it be like if we took a shower together? I'm really torn. Do you do it or do you not? Calabasas was no help—the girls ran in packs, and to hear one pack talk, all the other packs were basically whores. Actually, most of them were like me, complete virgins.

I finish the shower and slab on enough makeup to make Mom believe that I've decided to do it her way. But then I dress in a black, very severe Jil Sander dress that makes me feel good and bad, which is part of my love affair with Jil, I guess.

I have a heartbreaking day to endure with this ancient composer and his equally ancient lyricist. Back to Reynolds to do some songs he's probably had in a drawer since the days of Brandy. Brandy, the former star of *Moesha*, grew up into oblivion and that's what I fear is my fate.

"You look great," Mom says as I come into the kitchen and eat a strawberry Pop-Tart.

As so often before, I feel this intense love for my mother, despite the fact that I'm still angry about last night. I go over and kiss her on the cheek.

At first, there is no reaction. Then I realize she has stopped moving. Her hands clutch the countertop, her head is down, and her hair hangs around her face. I hear her quietly crying.

Suddenly we are in each other's arms and I'm saying I'm sorry and she's saying she's sorry, and we're bawling.

You cannot hate your mother for very long, at least I can't. In the limo, we sit hand in hand. This time, I don't get sick. This time, she does not smoke. We have, thankfully, left Mr. Dr. Shrink behind to water the plants.

We meet Jim Dexter at Reynolds, and his partner, Ray. Jim and Ray. They smile. I can see that they're happy for this work. I have a vision of a tiny apartment somewhere cheap, and them counting their change for food.

The first words out of my mouth stun me: "Could you do an arrangement of 'Nature Boy' for me?"

This sounds insane, even to me, but I know why I am saying it, and when Mom gives me a funny look, I just turn away.

Mom and I are not only mother and daughter, we are also business partners—and practically a married couple.

But we're business partners who don't trust each other. At the core, it's mom and kid, I guess, and that's where we always end up.

We go to work in a little acoustic studio with a piano. People like Elton John and Burt Bacharach have worked in this room, Jim tells me. At this very piano.

Ray is thin and shabby. He has taped glasses. There are nicotine stains between his fingers. He has a scar up the side of his throat.

He begins to play, and for the first couple of bars, I think maybe there's something there. But then it all falls apart into these god-awful cascades of arpeggios, and I cringe. It's agonizing.

I can see Mom knows as well as I do that these guys are a disaster. But we keep working anyway. We've paid them for the day, so we might as well get what we can out of them.

They will do the "Nature Boy" arrangement for me. Mom is suspicious, but she doesn't say anything except, "Since when did you take an interest in Nat King Cole? He's not your kind of sound at all."

All I can think of is those words from the song—"a very strange, enchanted boy." They go round and round in my head. Will he love me—or does he already—and will I love him in return?

I've thought about the fact that Nature Boy washes his hair

and he's clean and everything. So he must use apartments. My guess is that he totally owns the Beresford, and nobody knows he even *exists*.

On the way home, we show up randomly at the Ivy, which is, I think, Mom testing my star power. We're instantly seated. I get my usual scallops mini plate and Mom orders the lamb two ways. She says, "Bring me a Blue Label. Huge." I go into my iPhone while she buzzes away, wildly enthusiastic about the songs and the arrangements. My Twitter profile is active. At least my professional tweeter is awake. My last tweet was twenty minutes ago: "I'm so into my new songs. On a roll today!"

The meal passes, we come home, and Mr. Dr. Shrink is not waiting for us as I expected him to be. He appears to be like the others who show up around here, strictly gone tomorrow. Not even mentioned.

I've been lying in my room in the dark for fifteen minutes, and there are *no* sounds of my boy. He is not in my wall, he is not in my ceiling. I miss him and I want him because frankly I was counting on going to sleep listening to him breathing in the wall, and waking up to find him beside me again.

You know how this feels? Exactly like waiting for Santa Claus when you're a little kid. Only my darling guy is no big fat Santa.

I've never felt so beautiful as I felt in his eyes. I want that again. I want it right now, and I'm tossing and turning. I *want him here.*

I go up against the wall and put my mouth to it. "Are you in there? Where are you? Because I want you to come back. Please, come back."

But ohmygod what if he's a crazy person? He could be anybody. I could be in terrible danger.

Mom knows he is here because I told her, and I know a major complaint was filed with the building, so this beautiful person is probably being hunted down because of me.

I think he's wonderful and strange and kind of like a poem. Could I love him? Maybe, but first I have to stop feeling sorry for him. Right now, that's what I feel. It's a good feeling but it's not love.

I look in the closet again. The walls behind my clothes, the ceiling, the floor under my shoe rack. No secret openings. My bathroom, same deal—no secret openings, and the vent is too narrow. Under the bed? Not there, and no trapdoor.

So he doesn't come in via my room. Could he possibly have a skeleton key? But how? We had our own locks installed, and most everybody else does, too. We have three doors that lead into the apartment through the den, the foyer, and the kitchen. All locked all the time.

Is there another way in, like maybe in the pantry?

I open my door, but carefully. If Mom is still in the living room, I'm not going out there.

She is, but she's asleep on the couch and looks kind of haggard now. I love the Wicked Witch of the West because she is often my *mother*.

I creep very quietly into the kitchen. Open the cabinet under the sink. There's a hole back in there, but it's no bigger than your fist, plus it has a screen in it. Cabinet by cabinet, I open them all. No secret passages. Plus, the pantry is too full. He couldn't come in through a door in the back of it because he would arrive covered with pasta and olive oil and Carr's Whole Wheat Crackers.

Mom's bedroom? I look again at the heap on the couch and go in. Her room is totally chaotic. *Much* messier than mine. I'm not insane on the subject, but I like things to be where they're supposed to be.

There are a whole lot of clothes in Mom's closet. Stuff I haven't seen before. Crunchy silks and satins, and a big fur. When is she going to wear a fur? This is LA, so it's never all that cold. It's all white and stuffed into a plastic sheath. I didn't even know she owned it. Anyway, who wears real fur?

I leave because this is ridiculous—he didn't come in through Mom's room, and if she wakes up and finds me snooping around in her territory, then what?

He has to be coming in through either the foyer closet or the den. Or the living room, but I can't search there now. So I look in the closet, which contains my red parka and some umbrellas and no sign of any trapdoor, hatch, or anything like that.

The den, then. The walls are fake paneling. Could he be coming in through the paneling under the bookcases—like, pulling a piece of paneling back, laying it aside, and crawling through?

He sure could. But how do I find that out? Maybe I can't, actually.

Where is my phantom boy?

This seems hopeless. I'll check the closet just for the heck of it, because I can. Here's all of Mom's old stereo equipment. Here's the ridiculous basket collection. Why were we into that, collecting antique Easter baskets? And the Monopoly, Risk, Diplomacy, and Mexican Train boxes—all the old, ancient games of our life. Even Chutes and Ladders. Oh, wow. I remember Daddy always lost, and it was so funny because he wasn't faking to let me win. He was just hilariously awful at it.

Now, look at that! There is a hatch. It's in the ceiling of the closet, above the shelf so you hardly notice it even if you look up to get a game. But it's there. It looks official, like some kind of equipment access hatch or something, which is probably exactly what it is.

I think that it's also the only other way to get into this apartment apart from the locked doors.

I've found it.

I go into the kitchen and get the step stool out of the pantry. Oh, he'd better be in there, or I am going to go *insane*. Mom's head is thrown back, and she's snoring. She was wobbly drunk when we came in and does not hold her liquor well.

I return to the den and set up the step stool.

The hatch is so neatly framed, it's obviously an access point that's part of the building. There is no lock on it that I can see. It's basically a painted board resting on a frame. I push on it— and it silently goes up. Of course, he probably uses it all the time, so he'd make certain it was smooth and silent.

The smell of the dead air of the crawl space causes a shivery thrill through my body. And, wow, what a weird person I am that a crawl space gives me literal shudders. It's dark up here. I am talking *cave* dark.

I need a flashlight. The tool chest? No. The kitchen.

I make yet another trip past comatose Mom and look in the junk drawer. Very good, the flashlight sort of works.

So, back past Sleeping Beauty. I close the den door.

I look up into the darkness and turn on the flashlight. First I see black pipes. It looks too crowded up there even to get in, but then I see how it could be done. And, in fact, if I just move my head a little, I see that behind the pipes there is a big clear area. Above it, the light shows some kind of junk that has been sprayed on the top of the space. Insulation, maybe. Hanging below it are three rows of electrical wires.

I am fairly strong, I guess, but pulling myself up is going to be really hard. I'm going to do it, I have to do it. Why doesn't he come back, darn it? I guess I sort of threw him out, didn't I? I'm such a moron sometimes, but I was scared because it was all just so different and not what anyone would expect.

"Hey, up there! *Pssst!* Are you there?"

Not a sound, so I get up on top of the step stool and stick my head into the crawl space, which is not very roomy. How can he live like this?

I pull myself up, struggling, trying to get my knee up to brace myself, kicking against the wall (crap, *shh!*), pulling myself a little more and then rolling a bit, and I'm up. I am in the crawl space. His space.

I shine my flashlight around, looking for something resembling a human shape.

Off to the right there is a darkness. I move over that way, keeping to the beams because I have no faith in the plaster ceiling I am crawling on. All I need is to fall through and land on Mom.

With my flashlight and the light from the den, which is now behind me, I can see a bit. So I crawl farther, and where there are no pipes or wires, it's actually possible to get around.

Ahead, I hear rock music. That's our next-door neighbor, the party girl. Then *bzzzz, scree, bzzzt!* Light comes up and there is a hissing sound, which I realize is one of the elevators. I hear voices, a woman telling a man good-bye. Then the elevator goes clicking and scraping off down its shaft.

I go over and look down and the shaft is HUGE. You can see light glowing out of the rooftop vents of the four elevators, which are moving up and down, and a couple of them look *really tiny* because this building is *T-A-L-L*.

How could I *ever* have stood so close to the roof's edge? Was it really just the night before last? Time is losing all meaning.

I shine my flashlight around—and, of course, my flashlight is so awful, it only shines about three feet. I move a bit, trying to see more. I have to let him know he can come back. He is in here somewhere—he has to be.

Not around here, though. And suddenly I'm not sure where I am. Is the elevator shaft still over to the right?

I back up. Careful, here. I find a narrow shaft. It's not big around, maybe three feet on a side, and there are all kinds of pipes in it. I don't know what they are—sewers, water lines, whatever.

This is the shaft behind my room wall—must be. But how ever does he stay in here? This is his world, his home—that's how. He is somewhere down in there, but there is no way I can climb down a floor. Not possible.

I decide to call him. I will shout. Maybe it'll be audible in my room and maybe in the party girl's apartment, but not with all that music.

"Hello!" I flick my flashlight on and off. "HELLO!" I do it again, on and off, on and off. "HELLOOOOO!"

Nothing. So I have to give up on this because climbing around in here is dangerous, obviously, and I am no longer the girl who was on the roof. I am a different girl because I have a phantom boy somewhere off in that darkness.

One more try: "HELLOOO . . . HELLOOO . . . HELLOOO!"

Echoes. The rock music suddenly gets turned way down. Uh-oh.

I am as still as death, barely breathing. And then I hear something—a slapping sound. Is it party girl coming out of her apartment to see what's going on?

I hear it again, louder, *slap, slap, slap.* Louder and louder and I think—is it—is it coming from below?

I lean over the edge and shine my light and, *oh, Jesus, there he is!* And look at *that,* he is climbing the pipes, levering himself up from one side to the other. It's just awesome and magical to see how he does this, moving up the shaft so fast he's like the wind. Graceful and agile, look at that, just *look* at that!

My stomach goes shivery as I watch him coming, his hair flying, his hands gripping the pipes, his muscles rippling in the dim light of my flashlight. He almost doesn't look human, he is so good at this, a dancer of immense strength and power, a beautiful dancer. Then he rises over the edge, pulls himself up, and he's beside me. I am looking into the most beautiful, innocent smile I think I have ever seen.

"Hi," I say.

"Hi," he says back.

We lie in the crawl space side by side, facing each other. He reaches over and lays his hand on my cheek. I close my eyes and feel its weight, feel it stroking my skin.

Should I say it? Should I tell him I'm crazy for him? I want to but— Why do I hold back? This is a once-in-a-lifetime moment of magic, and I can't ruin it with my analytical, practical brain.

"I love you," he says. His breath smells like a taco. So he was down there somewhere eating Mexican food.

"Thank you," I say.

Our eyes link in the almost dark.

I open my mouth a little. I'm waiting. I don't want to wait, but I will wait because I want him to do it, to take me in his strength and his gentleness.

He kisses me. Our lips are together, but it's clumsy. We part, laugh a moment, and then he rolls his eyes and tries again. This time it works. I just love his strength, the feeling of him holding me to him so tight and him all trembly and excited, and me, too. I am so excited, I am almost wild—as wild as he is—except he is no brute, and I am no cave woman. He's very gentle with me, looking at me now with wonder in his eyes, then kissing my face all over until I throw my head back and laugh.

He says, "I thought you didn't like me."

"I was scared," I say.

He looks at me with the kind of seriousness you see in the faces of little boys, and it's so endearing. So I kiss him again, longer, more intimately. Afterward I draw back and he remains very still, his eyes closed, his lips slightly parted. He's savoring me, and I know how he feels about me—it's written in his shadow-filled face. I am so happy that I feel like laughing and kind of, I don't know, bubbling up inside in some way that I can't quite put my finger on. He is ready for me, and I can sense that he is quietly hopeful, but this is not the time. We have to cherish this moment. I have to especially cherish him, because he is so innocent.

I want him with me, because I think what's happening between us matters, and I want to find out for sure.

"You have to come and live in our apartment."

"Where would I stay?"

"We have two more bedrooms."

He turns onto his back and puts his hands behind his head. He's considering this. Finally he asks, "How?"

"*How?* Just come in and use whichever one you'd like."

"Oh, yes."

"Let me ask you this. Have you ever been out of this building?"

"No."

"Never? Never ever?"

"Not since Dad got killed. Luther held me over the edge. Luther wants me dead, too."

"Who is Luther?"

"Luther. That's all I know."

The quiet sadness in his voice reveals his grief.

Then I hear a noise. The sudden stillness that envelops him tells me he heard it, too.

"What is it?"

He doesn't reply. He's listening to something I cannot hear.

All of a sudden and without the slightest warning, a light shines on me.

From behind it, I hear Mom's voice say, "You must be psychotic."

I just scream. I scream and I scream, and I cannot stop screaming. He tries to comfort me, holding me, fluttering his hands at me, his face a pale image of agony.

Then *more* light—this time, shining directly at him—and his face is white as if glowing, his eyes bright with shock, his teeth bared, and I can hear him go, *"Aah! Aaah! AAAH!"*

The person shining the light on him is on top of an elevator that has risen up and stopped.

"Okay, young fella, don't try anything. I've got a gun."

My boy's eyes meet mine, and it's as if all of his heart is in those big eyes of his, now looking at me with terror. He grabs me for a second, lets me go, and then heads toward the equipment shaft.

"Stop or you're dead, kid."

So calm, so matter-of-fact, and not a cop, either, because no cop would ever say anything like that.

He is in the shaft now, and I try to go to him. I see the black maw of it and I know that it's death, and I think maybe I should just go with him, just drop down into the dark forever.

The man grabs my shoulder like some kind of iron monster, digging into me. The pain makes me shriek—and then my beautiful boy drops. Oh my God, he just *drops*.

But then I hear his *slap, slap, slap, slap* fading downward.

I turn and crawl toward the light my mother is shining in my face, and I go back down into the real world with her.

In the den, she grabs my shoulders and glares at me. "Did he touch you?"

"Go to hell!"

She cuffs my head, and I run out of the den and into my room and lock my door. Let her think what she wants. I go to my big windows and look out over the city, thinking of my beautiful boy and wondering if I will ever see him again.

That evil man's words ring in my memory: "I've got a gun."

Was it Luther? I couldn't see who it was 'cause of the bright light shining in my eyes. Well, whoever it was, he sure sounded like he meant what he said. I've got a feeling that he'll not only kill my sweet boy if he can, he'll enjoy every minute of it.

CHAPTER 11

To save himself, he had to leave her behind, that was crystal clear. She could never run a chase like he could. He saw her angelic face go flashing away as he dropped down the shaft, slapping against the pipes that lined it to break his fall.

When he was maybe five floors down, he stopped. It was nice and dark. He felt safer. But then there was a whining noise and something came zipping down from above—a cable!

A second later, light was beaming on him again, and with a terrifying screaming sound, a human form sped down the wire.

It was mountain-climbing equipment. He knew a lot about it; he'd seen it on TV and wanted it.

He dropped so fast that he almost lost himself, but then he managed to clutch a pipe. Again he went down, faster and faster, farther and farther, until the floors were whizzing past. Then he stopped and threw himself onto one—he wasn't sure which—and went skittering off into its crawl space, as far from the shaft as he could go.

The light came flashing, and he pressed himself down between two beams, praying that the ceiling he was lying on would not give way. Slowly, the light worked its way back and forth, back and forth, coming closer and closer.

Beresford began moving toward one of his hatches. A moment later, he heard grunting and scraping. *The man was almost on him.*

But a hatch was just two feet away. He opened it and looked down into a foyer closet. Who was this?

Oh, yes, he could tell by the smells of floor wax and cigarette smoke. This was Mrs. Scutter's apartment. He dropped down into the closet and pulled the hatch closed above him.

All he cared about now was being with Melody, but how could it ever work? *It would work; it had to.*

He couldn't plan, not now. He couldn't think ahead even ten seconds. He just wanted to feel her in his arms again— that was all he cared about.

His ability to listen was made acute by a life lived mostly in darkness. Beresford heard the man blundering in the crawl space, cursing and muttering. His pursuer wouldn't get far— he was too big.

He stood, barely breathing, as the man kept working his way closer to the hatch above. Despite the danger, he had only one thought: *Melody, Melody, Melody.*

At first, when the dog started barking, he thought it must be somewhere else because Mrs. Scutter didn't have a dog. But, no, it was right outside the door, and it was barking and barking and barking! So now she did. A new dog.

"Now, *now*, Buddy! Oh, goodness, what's come over you?"

The last three words were uttered in a tight, scared whisper. He could feel Mrs. Scutter looking straight at the door. He heard movement, then her whispered voice: "Operator, this is Elaine Scutter, apartment 4250 at the Beresford. I have an intruder—my dog has him cornered in a closet. Please hurry!"

Overhead, the hatch opened. "Okay, son, I've got you."

The light glared down on Beresford, and he burst into Mrs. Scutter's foyer.

The dog was not big, but it jumped almost up to his neck, snarling and snapping, and he had to grab it and hold it away from him.

"God, don't hurt me! Don't hurt me!" Mrs. Scutter lurched away, spit flying with her screams.

Then Frank tore out of the closet, filthy with dust, breathing hard, a long black flashlight in one hand and a bright silver gun in the other.

"All right, you bastard—"

But Beresford was already out the front door and running. He was not often in the halls like this, and he hammered at the elevator buttons until he realized that, of course, the elevators would be too slow. But then how, where?

The exit stairs, of course. With Frank right behind him, he ran to the door at the end of the hall. His first impulse was to go up, to hide in his place on the roof, to hide there forever. But he couldn't do that—he'd lead Frank right to his one safe place.

So he went down, leaping a whole flight at a time, his old T-shirt billowing as he raced faster and faster, with Frank pounding along behind him.

Then the pounding stopped.

Beresford also stopped. He listened . . . and heard breathing—*way closer* than he'd thought possible.

Instantly he started running the stairs again, the gun went *whang*, and he felt something sting the right side of his face. Plaster dust. Frank had shot at him!

He leaped over railings to get from one flight to the next, going down and down, until he reached the bottom of the stairwell.

Now he was in the subbasement. Like all the hidden parts of the Beresford, he'd been here before. But where to hide—what place would be absolutely secure? Because this was death that was coming for him.

"Melody," he said in his heart, "if I die tonight, my last thought will be of you."

He went along the catwalk above the machinery floor, then through the steel hatch into the fuel storage area with its three huge tanks. His plan was to get between two of them and lie there until they gave up looking for him, however long that took.

Then, somehow, he would go back up to fifty, and he would go to Melody and be with her forever. Somehow!

He didn't have it thought out; he just wanted it to happen. It *had* to happen. Love deserves to live—it's good and it's right. He needed her with him always, and she needed him. He had seen her face as he dropped down away from her, seen the sorrow in her perfect eyes.

It was inky dark in the fuel storage area, but he knew just where to find the space between two tanks, and after opening the hatch he slid into it.

Here, there was no sound except his own breathing. Or, no, that wasn't quite true. There was something else—a high, whining sound. But what could it be?

He listened more closely and realized it was coming from

just behind his back, out of the place where the two tanks touched each other. What would be whining like that? It sounded like a very small electric motor.

Then he heard a metallic *clunk*. Somebody had opened the door into this room. The next second, the light came on, yellow and far away, but light nevertheless.

"Now I've got you, and I'm gonna kill you slow, bastard. Down here where nobody's gonna hear, you goddamn *freak*!"

Frank came along the catwalk, his heels clinking on the steel grid. Beresford slid farther back into the shadows between the two tanks—where he felt something press against his back, something that should not be there. The whining sound was louder, also.

There was some sort of small machine tucked in deep between the tanks.

Frank was looking in this very space. Beresford squirmed back as far as he could go.

Frank stopped. With a soft grunt, he bent down and shone his light almost to Beresford's feet.

Beresford turned his head and saw the thing making the whining sound. It consisted of what looked like two big red candles with wire around them and a small black box between. It was this box that was doing the humming.

But what was it? He wasn't certain. Some kind of electrical

machine, but what were those big candles doing attached to it?

It should not be here, he knew that, and it looked like it might be dangerous—but then a light was shining straight into his face and he couldn't think about it anymore.

"You are good, you little shit. You are real good."

Beresford said nothing. All he could think about was somehow escaping, but he couldn't escape, and he had the sickening, stomach-burning feeling of being absolutely trapped.

"Come outta there or I'll blow your goddamn head to pieces!"

The gun clicked.

An image of Melody came into Beresford's mind, of her eyes, the depth of them, when she looked at him as they were starting to kiss.

If he came out from between the tanks, somehow maybe he would be able to break away from Frank and live to see her again. Staying where he was, he would die.

Stretching himself, wriggling forward, he crawled into the light.

"Get on your feet."

He stood up.

Frank looked him up and down. "Well, I'm damned. You're a specimen, you are. You a juicer? You got guns like a juicer."

Beresford was silent. He had no idea what Frank meant.

"Okay, come on, muscle boy."

Come where? How?

There came a blow to the side of his head that knocked him almost off his feet and sent a bright yellow flash through his left eye. He stumbled along the floor, then Frank jammed the gun into the small of his back and said, "Go up the damn stairs. Do it!"

Beresford took the stairs three at a time, thinking that he might—just might—get out the door and escape Frank again. Beresford had already realized that he was stronger than Frank, and he thought he might also be faster.

"Don't even think about it," Frank said, coming up behind him and pressing the gun into his back. "A bullet's a lot faster even than you."

Frank grabbed the back of Beresford's T-shirt in his fist and pushed him through the door.

With Frank prodding him along with the gun, he soon found himself at the back door of the building. Often he had wondered what lay on the other side. It was just beyond this door that Daddy had landed. So it was a sad place for him, a very sad place.

More than once, he had stood here crying. Over the years the door had seemed to get smaller and smaller, but he would never forget it as it first appeared to him, huge and ominous.

"Go on," Frank said, and pushed him with the gun.

His memories of being outside the building were very vague. Green grass, bright in the sun. His mother in a white dress. A dog named Prissy biting the water coming out of a hose. His dad's laughter, big and loud and happy.

The alley was silent. Up against the building, there was a long row of dark green Dumpsters stinking of garbage.

"Go on. We're going out to the street. Take it slow."

Beresford was shaking so much he couldn't control himself. The noise from all the cars shooting past hurt his ears. There was another sound, and it was getting louder: sirens.

He saw a gleam in one of the Dumpsters. A broken bottle. If only he could scare Frank with it, he could get back in and be okay. He could hide better. Someday, maybe even Frank would give up.

He could be near Melody, and somehow love would help him.

He glanced at the bottle. He was closer to it now. In another three steps, he could reach out and grab it.

The sirens were louder.

"Move it!"

The pistol poked into his back. He grabbed the bottle and whirled around. Frank jumped back, snarling.

Police cars came screaming into both ends of the alley, and Frank stuffed the gun in his pocket. "He's got a weapon," Frank shouted.

"DROP YOUR WEAPON AND LIE FACEDOWN ON

THE GROUND!" came a huge voice, echoing up and down the alley.

But the way to the door was now clear. So Beresford obeyed part of the order—he dropped the bottle. In three steps he was in the door, but there were footsteps and a man in a uniform but with no gun was there, and then Frank was coming in also.

"Careful, Joe, he's a monster!"

Joe stepped aside as Beresford went past. He needed to go up this time, to get to the foot of one of the shafts and climb into the heights of the building. But then more lights came on and the door into the lobby opened. A whole bunch of cops crowded into the narrow corridor and tackled Beresford.

He fought, pushing one of them aside and then another, slowly working his way closer and closer to the entrance to the equipment room, where all the shafts came out. But finally they had his arms and legs, and he was upended and being carried into the open space of the lobby, where the lights were blazing and there were more people than he had ever seen.

He struggled, he fought, but there were just too many of them, and despite his strength, he ended up in steel cuffs.

"He's just a kid, a big kid."

"Hey, kid, take it easy. You're gonna be fine."

"Man, he's pale as a damn fish."

"You stay in here, kid? You ever go outside?"

"Get him on his feet, but be careful."

Mrs. Scutter was there, and she shrieked, "He tried to kill me! He was going to rob me!"

As they took him out the front door, he craned his neck, looking for Melody but not seeing her anywhere.

But then he heard a cry, unmistakable, her voice in the crowd, *her voice*!

"Melody! Help me! Help me!"

"Wait! Give him to me!"

The crowd fell silent. One of the police said, "Miss McGrath?"

Then her mother was there and Julius, her bodyguard, and they swept Melody away, and Beresford called out to her—he called again and again—but she did not come back. Then he was in a strange little cabin with wire all around and a policeman beside him. The world was rushing past him, and he could not understand what he was seeing. The room was bouncing, flashing by, all blurred, none of it making much sense. He threw himself against the window, trying to get out.

"Jesus Christ, he's like a damn animal!"

Beresford felt himself being grabbed—his arm—

"Cool it, damn you! Stop the car, Jake, *stop the car*!"

The outside came into focus again, and Beresford settled down, once more looking for some way to get back to the building. But the building was gone.

Then they clicked more locks behind him, and the cop got out and went in the front on the other side of the wire. The space started moving again, and Beresford tried to get out and run, but his hands were cuffed behind him. No matter how hard he tried he could not move, so he yelled and tried to bite them and growled, but they just sat there.

"Okay, we got—we don't know what we got. Possible fifty-one fifty. Probable minor. We're gonna need social, and we're gonna need restraint on him big-time."

"You think he's a nutcase?"

"What're you, blind?"

"Just askin'."

This made more sense. This sounded like the way cops talked on *Law & Order*.

"I'm not blind," Beresford said.

"Hey, it can talk. Hey there, kid, take it easy. We're just runnin' you into juvie. Piece-a cake. Get you all squared away."

"You like hot dogs, kid? How long since you had a decent meal?"

"I had spaghetti." Earlier he'd eaten at the Neimans', a can of Chef Boyardee Forkables that had been in their pantry so long they'd never miss it.

"You'll get a square in juvie. How old are you?"

He didn't answer. He didn't want them to know that he wasn't sure.

"What's your name?"

Silence.

"You don't know your name?"

"We got some kinda problem child deal here, be my guess."

"There's a possible violent offense."

"You got ID, son? Driver's license?"

Beresford was not sure what he was supposed to say, so he said nothing.

The car stopped, and they unchained him.

"Now, stay calm, okay? 'Cause we don't want to make you walk around in chains. I mean, just take it easy. Nobody's gonna hurt you. We're your friends."

The other cop said, "Come on, now. Come on out."

"Man, this is the original wild child we have here."

"You got that right."

"Go in and push him out. Go in the other side."

Beresford understood that they wanted him out of the car and standing on the ground like they were. So he did as they said.

"Hey, he's gettin' with the program. Yes! Come on, kid, this here is Westview. You're gonna spend the night here."

"Not if he ain't charged. Violent offenders only."

"Well, that super is going to make sure he gets charged. He's gonna want him to stay in the system and not get back in their damn sewer pipes."

They took him across a parking lot with big lights every-where. He was trying to understand where he was and where the Beresford was so he could go home as soon as he got the chance. But it was all very confusing. There was a noisy, flashing mass of lights and swinging glass doors, and then he was in a room where there were other kids, a girl sitting hunched on a bench, a boy with orange hair who kept saying, "This is crazy, man, this is crazy," and other kids who eyed him like they wanted to maybe cut him up and eat him.

For a long time, he waited on a bench. The light was bright, the fluorescent bulbs the brightest he'd ever known.

As he waited, he examined his surroundings, thinking of only one thing: how do I get out of here and go back to where I belong?

There was a drop ceiling, but he knew that the crawl space would be no good. The ceiling was suspended from a metal frame like in the security room. If you tried to get up in there, the whole thing would come down.

The building was low, so there were no long chases to get through. He looked at the air-conditioning ducts for a while, wondering if they offered a way out. They were just about big enough, so the only thing to do would be to try.

"Okay, son, we don't have any identification on you, do we? Could you state your name, please?"

He had figured out what he would say: "I'm Mr. Beresford."

The lady, who wore a blue uniform and had complicated braids, wrote on a clipboard. Then she looked up at him. "Your name is the same as the building? Whaddayou, own it?"

He did not know what she was asking, so he remained silent.

Finally she said, "C'mere, come with me."

She unlocked him. They went to a desk where a man sat writing. "This isn't a violent offender. I think it's a mental case, so he goes to Social Services. No ID. Told me his name was the building he's been squatting in. What you got here is a homeless teenager. Looks like he's been in the wind for a while."

"He's not hurtin'—look at 'im. Healthy kid."

"Yeah, he's got a good crash somewheres."

Beresford decided that the ductwork was his best chance.

"Son, how old are you?"

The questions were beginning to buzz in his mind like a plague of flies. He couldn't take them much longer.

"Where were you born?"

"Just a moment." The lady stepped across the room, then came back with a stack of cards. She held one up. "Read this."

It was words. He did not know what it said. He did not know how it worked, not with big words like that, big long ones.

"That is the word *train*. Do you know what a train is?"

He'd seen the trains down in the railyard. South side of the building, look down and out, they were there. "They are in the railyard."

"Henry, this boy is nearly illiterate, and he doesn't know

his own name or age, and he has no identification. What have we got here?"

"Well, I'll tell you one thing we got is a charge sheet." He picked up a sheet of paper. "This boy is getting charged. Breaking and entering and theft of services. The complainant is the Beresford 123 Apartment Corporation. Next, attempted robbery and attempted assault. Complainant is a Mrs. William Scutter." Henry put down the paper. "They don't want him back, that's for sure."

"We'll isolate him. He's not gonna survive the population."

Beresford did not think that the window glass was too thick to break, and he was just considering throwing himself through it when they led him into a little room where a lady with a cheerful voice said, "You're going to get your picture taken, pretty boy. Smile, now."

He did as he was told.

She laughed. "Now, that is about the biggest smile I've ever seen in here. You're one happy defendant."

They fingerprinted him, which he knew about from TV. He also knew that they were going to put him in jail, because that's where this kind of stuff led, and he needed to get out of there before they did that. He could not escape the bars of jail, and the idea of being trapped like that, of not being able to get back where he belonged, of never seeing Melody again—he could not think of these things very long without his mind starting to roar.

There was only the one person in this room, and he saw an air-conditioning vent, so he jumped up and pulled off the grate.

"My God! You come down from there!"

He slid into the duct and went a few feet. Behind him, there was a lot of yelling, and he knew that they were trying hard to get him and bring him back. Sweat poured off him, and he used it to lubricate his way when he came to a turn. Getting his body around it pulled muscles in his neck and chest so tight he thought they might rip, and he had to suck breath through his teeth to keep from screaming with the pain.

Voices boiled up from below, and then there were thuds and clanks and the sound of scraping as somebody pulled away ceiling tiles. He moved more easily now, and quickly, turning another corner and going down to the far end of the wide building. Navigating by sound, he went toward the machine room.

Soon he was in a larger duct and a lot of air was coming toward him. The darkness was absolute, so he felt his way ahead carefully, until his hands met an edge.

There was a crashing noise, and light flooded in behind him. They'd broken into the ductwork. So he had to do this, and he had to do it now. But what? How?

"It's been tried, son. It don't work."

The voice was right behind him; he felt a hand around his ankle.

"You go down there, you gonna get cut up by that fan. Don't make a mess like that, son. It's nasty cleanin' up."

Now there were hands on both his ankles, and he was being pulled back. Frantic, he pressed against the walls of the duct.

"Dammit, it ain't no use, spider boy."

He was dragged back and into the light.

"I got him, I got him—don't let this thing fall, man!"

The ductwork sagged and groaned, but it didn't break as the big man brought Beresford out.

"We gonna get you tucked in nice and tight, spider boy. You a piece-a work, you are."

They were in a room full of desks. There were strange green walls with markings on them, some of which were letters and others numbers. He could read a few of the words—*red, big, July*—but most of them were too long.

As they led him out, somebody hit him on the head from behind.

"You give us trouble, we give you trouble. It's an eye for an eye around here, spider boy."

They went down a long hallway, its walls painted dirty green. There were doors every few feet, with narrow glass windows embedded with wire.

"Okay, put him in twenty-one."

"You wanna do that?"

"He's violent—he tried an escape. You're damn right I want to do that."

"Because he's harmless."

"Harmless? We got a good five grand of ductwork and ceilings to think about. That ain't exactly harmless."

The man used a circular key that Beresford knew was a very difficult one to unlock the door. When it opened, there was a sharp smell of human bodies, and he saw eyes peering at him from bunk beds. There were six of them, and two of the uppers were empty.

"Okay, girls, you got a new roomie. He ain't got no name, so don't ask him. And he don't talk a whole lot."

"Hey, man, he a ghost. We don't want no ghost in here."

"Shut up. And if he gets into a squabble, nobody's listening."

"What he do to you, man?"

"He troubled me, Louis. He troubled me very much."

They left and closed the door, and Beresford heard it lock.

"What you doin' in here, ghost? What you do?"

"I need to get back to my building," he said carefully.

"You *need* to get on your knees, ho, that's where you *need* to get."

Beresford looked at this boy, who had come up out of a lower bunk. He had short red hair and eyes unlike any he'd ever seen. They were the eyes not of a person but of a very smart animal. Beresford wasn't sure what this meant, but he was sure he was right. He felt a huge sadness for this boy and thought, he has been made this way by somebody very mean.

The boy came face-to-face with Beresford. He had good muscles and a metal band of some sort in his lip. "Go down, ho."

The others in the room were silent, watching.

Beresford decided that he would not kneel down. Why this boy wanted him to he did not understand, not exactly, but it was not good—that he did understand.

Then the boy's fist came up and, before he could block it, struck a shattering blow to his head.

There was a flash. The world floated silently away, and all became dark.

CHAPTER 12

Frank's phone rang. He was exhausted. He'd been up all night getting rid of the evidence that the damn kid might have seen.

"Hello?"

It was Szatson.

"Yes, sir?"

"What's with this wild child?"

"Excuse me?"

"'Wild Child Found in Exclusive Downtown Apartment Building.' You damn jerk, this is all we need, drawing this kind of attention to the building just now." As he said the last two words, his voice dropped down. *Just now.* Concealed in them, Frank knew, was the terrible secret the two of them shared.

"He's in juvenile custody."

"I figured that out. You knew what needed to be done, and it wasn't done, was it?"

"Sir, I didn't have—"

"Don't hit me with excuses. You did not do your job."

Frank had never killed anybody, and to tell the truth, he'd been glad when the cops got that kid. Even worse was the idea of killing this building. Every time a tenant said something to him, in the back of his mind was the thought that this person was probably going to burn to death or be a jumper, and it would be on his head.

Now the intercom buzzed. Frank jabbed at the button and Linda, the day concierge said, "There's a couple of detectives up here."

His stomach gave a sick turn. The last thing he needed.

"What is it? What's she saying?"

"Bulls."

"You *jerk*!" Szatson slammed down the phone.

Frank feared that Szatson would send a gun over here. Frank might have a hard time with murder, but he doubted Luther Szatson did.

He'd cleaned up the fuel storage area, of course, but the kid had been in the worst possible place, right in there next to the device. Had he seen it? Had he understood what he was seeing? Had he told the cops—and was that why they were here?

At four o'clock this morning, he had dropped the remains of the incendiary device off the Santa Barbara pier.

"Frank?" It was Linda again.

"I'm coming!"

"Stay there. They're on their way down."

At that moment two LAPD detectives came in the door, one a short, Italian-looking guy, his hands nervously exploring his narrow jaw. The other was taller and solemn, with a sad, beaten sort of a face.

"We just have a few routine questions," the tall man intoned.

"Okay."

"The thing is, this kid that came out of here—he's—we're stumped. He's not in any database. We can't even get a name out of him."

"I don't know a thing about him."

"Which is what you said last night to the uniforms, sir, and that's fine. But he must have a room in here somewhere. There must be something for us to see."

The other detective added, "We can find out a lotta things. We just need access to his room."

"Look, I've been trying to figure that out. Where the hell did he stay? My employer wants an answer, too."

"I'll bet."

"Because what if I've got a whole damn colony of homeless in here? It's a big place. To make a long story short, me and my security guys, we went through every vacancy in the structure this morning and didn't find so much as dust out of place."

"So he was here but he wasn't? The juvies say he looks like a mushroom. He's been indoors for months."

"Unless he roomed with somebody who hasn't come forward, then I don't know how he managed." He was about to add that he'd found him in a crawl space with Melody McGrath, but decided to keep his mouth shut about that. Any cop would turn right around and sell that to the media, and the place would be overrun again.

"Look, Social Services will keep hassling us until we get something. They don't like nameless orphans—it screws up their paperwork."

"I thought there were charges against him. So he stays inside, right? No matter who he is."

"You can process an adult unidentified, just John Doe him and forget it. But not a minor. A minor, it's all different."

"You know he's a minor? You know that?"

"The medical staff at Westview made that determination, yes. He's between fifteen and seventeen. He is a minor."

If they had a name, they'd go away. But Frank was afraid to just make one up. As soon as they found out it was no good, they'd be back, and they'd have more questions, harder ones, and some would be about him.

The phone rang again. He snatched it up.

"Where is he?" It was a female voice, young—and familiar.

"Excuse me?"

"Let me tell you something. You might work hand in glove with my mother. You might suck up to her, but you *will* suffer for what you did. Damn you!" And then *click*.

He did not need that little fireball on his ass, that was for sure.

The detectives were watching him. They looked like a couple of poured-out old doofuses, but that, he knew from too much experience with detectives, was just a shtick. The thing about detectives was that until they suspected someone, they suspected everyone. They were never without suspicion, not the good ones, and the LAPD had a lot of good ones.

"If there's anything else I can help you with?"

For a moment, they both stared at him in silence. Finally, the tall one unfolded himself and stood up. "We'll get it figured out," he said. "It all comes together in the end, am I right?"

They left, wandering off down the hall, seemingly oblivious but, he felt sure, taking everything in. They'd be suspicious as hell now. They'd assume that he was concealing something, because how could this kid have been in here without being noticed?

When they went after Frank's records in the system, what happened then? If there was the least thing wrong with whatever paperwork Szatson had used to get him released, there was gonna be a world of trouble coming his way.

He opened his bottom desk drawer and took out the bottle of vodka he kept there. Took a big swig, then again.

The phone rang. Szatson. Dammit.

"Mr. Szatson, may I help you?"

"Get over here now—we need to talk pronto."

Frank hung up, took two more long pulls on the bottle, and left.

He drove the streets almost blindly, trying to convince himself that the thing to do was to just keep driving. Head east, maybe to Vegas. You could get lost there, live on odd jobs. There was always something to do in Vegas, if you were willing to work the bottom.

Problem was, if he went into the wind now, the detectives would certainly follow.

He went up Szatson's driveway, stopped for the entrance gate, then parked his old Plymouth. For a moment, he sat still, trying to get his mind to slow down. He was gonna be raked over the coals here. He needed his wits about him.

Szatson pulled the door open.

"Frank, this is a mess."

"It got away from me." He followed Szatson into the dark, silent cavern of a house.

"Let's get it fixed," Szatson said.

"Mr. Szatson, I collected the materials that—"

Szatson turned on him. "That what?"

"That the kid saw."

"Goddammit! And you're certain of this?"

"We have to assume it."

"And he's in the juvenile system."

"He's at Westview, transferring tomorrow to the Willamette Camp above Los Feliz."

"Well, then let me ask you another question. Can you handle it?"

"There's nothing for me to handle. He's gone. He's in the system."

"Frank, do you understand how much money is involved here?" Szatson asked.

He nodded.

"A whole world of money. Money that is *obligated*." Szatson fingered what appeared to be some sort of college ring. "All over the world. Russia, China, Myanmar."

If people in places like that didn't get repaid, they killed you. So Mr. Szatson was in danger, too.

"We need to get this done, Frank," Szatson added. "I'm giving you a chance to fix it, but understand that it's a last chance."

Frank nodded. But he still didn't understand. "Fix it how?"

"Do the damn kid! Reach in there and do him!"

Was this possible? Of course it was. It was always possible to hit somebody on the inside.

"You don't need to worry about the kid," Frank said. "The kid is finished."

"When?"

He would have to reach into juvie, which meant going to the gangs. He had some connections there, guys who did fires for him.

"Couple days."

"Tonight, damn you! No later."

He nodded. So he was committed to his first murder, and the most dangerous kind. Hits went wrong. People sang to save themselves from hard time.

"Tonight," he said. "For sure."

Chapter 13

You never forget a boy who touched your soul
  but had to go.
Your heart follows him until it's lost.
But you'll never stop, no matter the cost.

I have to get him out. I have to get him back. But I still don't even know where he is, and I have no name! I think I'm going to go totally insane here.

I want him. I can help him grow and become a real person. He is so innocent and vulnerable, and I am so upset that my brain is buzzing with images of him being beaten up or screaming his lungs out in some cage. I don't think I can bear another night of the sleepless hell I endured last night.

I tell myself, "Girl, you hardly know him—he's some kind of a freak who lives in walls," but then I remember the joy sparkling in his eyes when he looked at me, and I think love that pure has value.

Innocence like his is almost unknown in this world, and to touch it as I have is an incredible privilege. I want to take him in my arms and make him safe. And I can, I know I can. If only I can find him.

And yet, work goes on. My concert is Saturday night, *this Saturday night*! I look at my MySpace and Facebook pages—they are swarming. Speculation. Anticipation. The story of Mom's freakathon over my music is all over the place.

One thing, Mom is aware of her mistake. Today we went up to the Greek for rehearsal, and she didn't have her sweet old composer there to feed me ditties. Of course she ruined all my scratch tracks, so my music won't be available for download and the album is delayed six weeks, but at least it will be my music, my real music.

The *People* reporter got right to her blog and went all hissy, and, guess what, now my fans want my music as never before. Mom as the Wicked Witch of the West is laughing all the way to the bank. She staged that one brilliantly.

If it's to ensure my success, Mom isn't afraid to make me hate her. She isn't afraid to make my fans despise her. It's an act so good that even I believe it.

So, the Greek Theatre. I looked out off that stage and was amazed at how huge the Greek actually is. And get this: there were fans waiting for me when I came this morning for sound check—a couple hundred of them who had been hanging out there for hours just hoping to say hello.

I was supposed to be driven right up to the stage entrance, so their wait would have been for nothing, but Mom made the driver stop, and I got out and hung with them for a while. Julius was so nervous that he practically exploded. A couple of guys gave me phone numbers. Everybody who had the CD of my first album got it signed in metallic blue ink.

My fans made me feel better. Some of them look really fierce. Bikers. Gang boys. Go figure.

For a few minutes, I didn't think about him. But the second I was on that big, lonely stage, my mind went back to a torment of worry: Where is he? What's happening to him now? Will I ever see him again? And when? Last night I lay awake in bed just wishing that he would somehow escape and I would hear his breathing through the wall again.

If only I hadn't been scared of him. If only I hadn't complained to Mom, he would still be there and we'd have our little secret nest in the crawl space. No matter what happens to him, he will never return to life in the walls of the Beresford. I'll teach him about the world; I'll teach him everything he needs to know. I'll even hire him. He can be a roadie, and I'll get a tour bus, and we can live on it together between tours.

It's all a total fantasy, I know that. They will never let him out. The building will accuse him of all kinds of crimes, because Mom says the super told her he did robberies and all. I fear that our love will be, for him, a brief spark lost in the past. But for me, it will still be in my heart just as it is now.

The one good thing that has happened is that my band is coming together. We had some strong rehearsals today, and I had the added fun of watching Mom suck her plastic cigarette when I did "Flying on Forever." She hates that song the most because she thinks it's about teen suicide. I don't know. I just like being on the edge.

I've thought up a plan to save my beautiful boy. I disguise myself and pretend I am his mother. Yeah, right.

Another plan: I break into the juvie tank. I looked at it online, and this does not look impossible . . . for a professional safecracker or whatever.

When I got home, I had a frozen burrito for dinner—bad girl, slap your hand—it was cheesy and delish. I also drank a beer, which was great until I discovered that Kaliber couldn't put a buzz on a gerbil. Now that dear Dr. Singer has gone the way of all her other instant boyfriends, Mom has replaced his Chimay with something I could safely steal.

Okay, girl, you have to get with the program and stop coming up with ridiculous plans because you need to do two things: First, find him. Second, get him out of there.

I thought of calling our lawyers, but they would instantly call Mommy dearest, and then I would probably end up chained to my bed with duct tape over my mouth—except for rehearsals tomorrow and Friday, of course. And the concert. Oh, how amazing, *the concert*. The last one had, what, two hundred and fifty people? It looked great because the room was small. I know they call the Greek small, but that's not how it looks to me. It's this positive *ocean* and incredibly scary.

I'm all over the place. This is happening because I can't figure out a thing to do to help him. Except—what if I were to report him as a missing person? How do you do that? Is there a Web site? Or, no, you probably have to do it in person at the police station, which is where?

What if I just go to the big juvie facility in East LA and say he's my autistic brother? I'm his guardian, except I think you have to be twenty-one for that.

Maybe the thing to do is go down to the parking garage, get in the Mercedes, and drive over there. Except I've had my license since my birthday, which was less than twelve months ago, therefore I can't drive between eleven P.M. and five A.M.—thank you, California.

I could take a cab. Get there, talk my way in, get visitation. I know it says on the Web site no visitation, but maybe it's not all that cut-and-dried—you never know. Does money talk? Bet so.

I pull down my hair, wash my face totally plain, then put on my dark glasses. I look sort of like a vampire who's pretending to be me. I put on this Vincent Napoli lipstick, "It's Not Me," which is this sort of Goth-insane purple-black color. I hit my face with a bunch of white foundation, and now I look like some punk moron trying to do Angelina Jolie as if she was a punk moron.

Okay, heavy disguise and I am gone. Mom left a while ago, so hopefully she's reconnected with Dapper D or the Wolverine or whoever and is off playing house somewhere far away.

Julius is on call. Do they have something rigged up that lets him know if the door is opened? Probably, so I have to move fast.

I hit the hallway and run down four stories, then take the elevator, clever girl. As I go down, I hear the faint *whoosh* of the car beside this one going up.

"A cab. I need a cab, please."

"And you are?"

I lean close to the building attendant. Lower my glasses just a tad, look over them. "I'm Angie Jolie."

"Oh, wow! I mean, sure! Uh . . ."

Angelina Jolie would, of course, never need a cab, but the woman makes the call anyway, and I go out and sit on one of the benches, hoping that Julius does not—

"Hello, Mel."

"Hi, Jules."

"You goin' out?"

"Not to a public place, so you can go back to your room."

He sits down beside me. "We can take the Mercedes. I'll drive you."

Actually, it might work if he doesn't go apeshit on the spot. If I say the truth, either I'm ruined or I get my chance.

"Will you take me to juvie in East LA?"

"Where that streeter was taken?"

"He lived here! This was his home!"

"Whatever. Look, you got a thing for him, don't you? Your mother already ripped me about it, although she had to admit that I'm not gonna be able to monitor the crawl space."

"Take me, Julius, please!"

"You tell her we went to the Star Room, and it's a deal."

"Will she believe that, Jules? That I would go there, ever? I mean, they do the foxtrot there."

"She won't believe it. But she will believe me when I tell her it wasn't some rock-'n'-roll pharmacy like M&M."

So I agree to say I went dancing the foxtrot, and we get in the Merc to go to the juvie facility.

I am so incredibly happy until we arrive. Now what? What do I do—go in with my bodyguard and say I want to see a big blond kid with no name, the one who came out of the wall at the Beresford?

As Julius stops the car, he tells me, "You will see some real sad stuff in there, Mel. Saddest stuff you've ever seen, so be prepared. And don't bring me out a bunch of vagrant kids to feed, okay? Promise me."

"I promise."

Boy, is this place BIG. Plus it feels all courtlike and scary, and I see cops bringing in these two sweaty fat monsters in handcuffs with torn up T-shirts. One of them has blood on him and looks like he could eat the Incredible Hulk for din-din, which maybe he just finished doing.

I push the door open and there are these benches with kids sitting on them, and there is a big Latina beside her hunched-over daughter, who is crying, and Mom has a defiant look on her face, like her girl had to have been picked up by mistake or something. I hope that is true, but I bet it isn't.

I go up to a desk where there is a lady in uniform. She has a gun. Everybody in uniform here has a gun and a billy club. This is not a nice place in any way.

The lady is writing. She keeps writing. If I was a taxpayer, I'd be outraged.

"Ma'am, I am trying to locate a boy who was brought in last night."

"Family?"

"That's the thing—we're not sure. We read that he'd been taken from the Beresford and was unidentified."

She looks up. Now I wish I'd worn a nun's habit, not this ridiculous getup.

"Oh, man," she says. "Melody McGrath!"

Silence falls. I feel the eyes on me, all of them in the room. It's as still as the air before a storm.

"You know him, Miss McGrath? Because we got no ID on him."

"I may know him." I feel like a bird that has just discovered it is in a cage.

"Oh, hey, can you sign this for my son?" a guard asks. He has a napkin, which I sign with his Bic.

"He went into the system," the lady at the desk says. "He's at, um—actually, I shouldn't tell you this if you're not family."

"We don't know. If he's autistic, he might be."

She gives me a this-is-weird look, then goes into bureaucratic mode. "They took him over to Willamette. The charges didn't go with him, so he's gonna get fostered."

I tell her thank you and turn and give two more autographs. The girl who was hunched over watches me with the most incredible longing, and I know what's in her mind: "If only I was you."

Back in the car, I tell Julius, "He's at Willamette." Then I ask, "Do you know where that is?"

"Silver Lake. But it's a camp. They have visiting hours at those places."

"Will you take me?"

"If your mom allows it, sure."

"Then forget it. Because she won't."

"You have your live run-through tomorrow. When it's over, we can do a detour."

"She'll be in the car."

"She'll be in the limo. I'll come separately."

He can be such a doll, but when I really think about it,

what will they do for me at Willamette that didn't happen at Westview? They're not going to help me. Going to these places isn't the way to succeed, here.

"Thanks, but let's just forget it."

At home I lie back on my bed and think. He is in there. I am out here. He has to be very scared and confused. I mean, he doesn't know much of anything.

What if I could identify him for them? Find out his name?

Maybe he has a place on the roof. That night he found me up there, he hid back in the shadows near the water towers.

One second later, I am in the hall with my flashlight in hand. Julius is probably downstairs in his room watching me on a camera and saying to himself, "Doesn't this kid ever stop?" Since I got caught with the boy, he has orders to check on my every move. (The hatch into the crawl space is gone, plastered over while we were in rehearsal.)

I go to the stairs and up to the roof.

It's big and beautiful and easy to imagine that you're on a magic carpet flying above this astonishing sea of lights. The Beresford is fifty stories tall and on a hill, so I think it's about the highest building in downtown.

I look for his place. It has to be small and well concealed.

Up close, the air-conditioning towers are massive, and there is a humid, old-water smell to them. I'm not sure how building air-conditioning works, but up close this is really impressive and daunting. Could I get hurt getting too close? Is it electric? But no, it's full of falling water.

Back here, this is where he came out of, definitely.

I shine my light along the opposite wall, which must be some kind of storage or equipment room. I see nothing . . . until I do. There, down there, is a long crease, black. Looks like a shadow until I go closer. Shining my light in, I can see that it's like a low, narrow hatch. There is no handle, so I pull at it but I can't get a grip. I push, but it doesn't move inward. Then I slide my fingers along the edge, which is so fine that without the flashlight I never would have seen it.

I push the top edge. Nothing. Then the bottom edge. It levers out a little at the top. I pull at the exposed sliver, and it comes down.

To see in, I have to lie flat on the roof. I shine my light into this very small chamber. It's maybe seven feet long, three feet deep, and three feet high. It's like some kind of shelf with a cover on it. Could have been a space for drills and things.

I'm highly claustrophobic, but I slide in anyway and look around. There are clothes stacked up at the far end, neatly folded. There are three bottles of water, an Evian and a couple of Poland Springs. There's a half-empty bottle of fruit punch Gatorade. On the wall, there's a picture of a woman. It's color, an old snapshot, tiny and wrinkled like it came out of a little boy's pocket, which I'm sure it did. She is thin, with blond hair like his. Standing beside her in the sunlight of another time is a happy-faced little boy, and I know with total certainty that it is him.

I can see a story here, of loss and abandonment, and although many of the pieces are missing, I can also see the tragedy of it, the little boy deserted during his father's murder, too scared to ask for help but smart enough to make this crazy, impossible place his home.

Looking at his little bit of stuff—the few clothes, the threadbare blanket—and thinking of his deep, pleading eyes, I know I am falling for him in a big way.

What I cannot see, though, is any sign at all of who he actually is. No name scrawled on the picture, no souvenir with an address on it, nothing.

It's so sad and so incredible. I turn over and grab his blanket, and I can smell him in it—the sadness of a boy alone. And I cry and I cry and I cry.

CHAPTER 14

On the third night of his captivity, Beresford was watching TV in the rec room at Willamette when he saw something that really scared him: a shot on *CSI* of a time bomb. It had a digital timer wired to three waxy, bright red sticks that looked like candles. For a moment he was confused, trying to recall where he'd seen this before. Then he remembered—there had been something that looked very much like it in the space where he'd hidden between two of the tanks in the Beresford's fuel storage area.

Before he could stop himself, he jumped up and cried out. He immediately stifled the sound, but not before a ripple of suppressed laughter filled the room. The other kids hated him. They called him "the vampire" or "zombie boy." He dropped back into his seat, but his mind was racing and his breath came in gasps.

He'd been focused on the kids since he arrived, on trying to figure them out. But this discovery devastated him. He had to get back to the Beresford. Somehow, he had to escape.

There was no point in telling the staff. They'd just think it was another one of his crazy attempts to get out.

He sat like a stone, staring at the TV but not seeing it. He needed a plan. Since his attempt to get out through the duct-work at Westview, they had kept him on tight lockdown, so he was in his own tiny cell at night. There was no way out—he'd explored every inch of it.

Sometimes kids got to go with their families on weekend nights, and maybe there was some sort of opportunity. He approached Mr. Lopez, a monitor on duty.

Finally Mr. Lopez looked up from the magazine he was reading. "Yeah?"

"Can I go to the Melody McGrath concert tomorrow night?"

"Whaddaya know, it talks! You ain't got a family to be signed out to, and with an escape attempt in your record, no judge would give you a home date anyway, even if you had one."

"My name is Beresford McGrath. I told everybody that."

"So ain't it strange that your momma, Mrs. McGrath, has no idea that she even gave birth to you? You can't just make up an identity, kid. An identity comes with a birth certificate and parents who know who you are—and a school record. You ain't got none of that. What you do have is a placement hearing coming up, so you got a court appearance Tuesday."

Beresford returned to his seat. He had to get back—that was all there was to it.

He knew that this place wasn't all one building, and when you went from building to building, you were outside. They watched you, though, every minute, and anyway the rec room where he was now was in his dorm, so he wouldn't be going out tonight.

Mr. Lopez was looking at him. Why? What was he thinking? He could never tell if somebody was mad or not. He didn't know how to tell. It was easy to insult people here, and maybe he'd insulted Mr. Lopez. But how?

"Hey, kid." Mr. Lopez nodded for him to come over, so Beresford went back to the desk.

"If you got a pass, where would you go? Just to that concert?"

At that moment, the bell rang and all the kids got up, suddenly very disciplined, heading for the wings of the building where the sleeping areas were. You could get a demerit for being slow on the bells.

As they congregated in front of the door to the boys' wing, waiting for it to be buzzed open, Beresford felt a hand slip around his waist. He jumped away and whirled around, but the faces of the kids behind him were all blank.

Could they get into his room? They hit the door and rattled it whenever they got a chance. Only the staff had keys, but what did that mean around here? The kids really ran the place.

Beresford went into his room and closed the door. With the familiar loud buzz, all the doors locked.

In the silence that fell, the situation hit him so hard he had to gasp for breath. There was a bomb in the Beresford. Who might do this he could not imagine, but it was there, no question. When would it explode?

He had to get out of here.

He paced back and forth, back and forth, slapping the door, slapping the narrow window, back and forth, back and forth.

Beresford thought about all the dogs and cats he comforted, the people who needed him, even mean old Mrs. Scutter—especially her, the way she was always falling asleep with lit cigarettes. He thought of Melody asleep in her apartment way up at the very top, and realized that when the explosion came, all the people on the top floors would be cut off and trapped.

He paced for a long time, he had no idea how long. Time was always kind of a surprise to him. He'd known night and day—but mostly night—in the crawls and chases where he'd lived. Sometimes on the roof he'd seen the sun, which was always disturbing because of how hard it made it for him to hide.

Finally, he felt sleepy and thought it was time to find a vacationer or go to his place on the roof—and then he remembered where he really was. He cried out, stifling it instantly with his fist.

Beresford lay down on the incredibly soft bed, then, as he had on all the nights he'd been here, took the blanket to the floor so he could sleep without feeling like he was falling. Melody had an even softer mattress. How could she stand it?

He lay staring up at the ceiling, at the faint reddish light that kept the room not quite dark. That was another thing he didn't like here. It was never totally dark. He was best in total darkness, even climbing and moving through the crawls. It was what he was used to. He could navigate just by sound and touch.

He must have fallen asleep without realizing it, because a sound woke him up. The door went *bzzt*! Hardly any buzz at all.

Was it morning? No, the window was black. He sat up. Why would they be opening the doors now? He stood and grasped the door handle. Gently, he pulled and pushed, but the handle did not turn. So maybe he'd dreamed it.

The door burst open. Four hooded figures came in and pushed him up against the far wall. As they did, he shouted in surprise.

"Shaddup! The bulls ain't comin'. The bulls gone deaf tonight."

One of the figures was Rufus the Butcher, a gang guy. In his hands was a length of wire.

Beresford had not used his real strength against them before, but he had to now, he saw that immediately. As Rufus raised his fists, the wire taut between them, Beresford shrugged off the two boys holding him, lifting one of them and throwing him into the ceiling. The boy hit hard, crashing to the floor in a heap of ceiling tiles.

"Jesus!"

Beresford waded into them, swinging his arms, hammering them. Strong as they appeared, to him they were like paper. A lifetime of climbing had turned his muscles to iron.

He grabbed Rufus by his T-shirt and landed the hardest punch he could throw right in the middle of his stomach. With a huge gasp, Rufus shot backward out the door and into the far wall, then slumped to the floor.

The other two started to run, but he caught up with them in the hall and hit their heads together, dropping them both. The one he had thrown into the ceiling was still knocked out on the floor of his room.

He did not like hurting anyone—he hated it, in fact—but that wire meant only one thing, that they were there to kill him. Then the place would go back on lockdown and nobody would be the wiser. That was how it happened here.

He went down the hall and out into the rec room. From here, he had to pass the front desk, but just as Rufus had said, nobody was there. To keep the peace, the guards cooperated with the gangs.

Why would the gangs want to kill him, though? He had nothing to do with them.

He pulled open the main door and smelled the air, rich, cool, and scented with night-blooming flowers. The world was beautiful in so many ways. He would never cease to feel this, not after all his years in concrete and darkness and dust.

He ran, dashing between the gym and classroom building and heading across the baseball diamond to the high fence beyond. He knew about maps, but the connection between the lines and the streets and roads did not make any sense. His instinct was to get high up; then he could see.

The lights on the baseball diamond were on, so he skirted it and climbed the twelve feet of chain-link fence, until he reached the vicious-looking razor wire at the top. He'd only seen this stuff from a distance, and he touched it in horrified amazement. How could anybody put up something as evil as this? It could cut a person to pieces. But it kept people like Rufus inside, and you sure didn't want him free, did you?

Beresford lifted his body on one arm, drew in his legs, twisted until his feet were facing the other side of the fence, then extended his legs through a gap in the wire.

Even for him, holding his entire weight on one arm was

hard, so he immediately grasped the fence with the other hand as well, then levered himself down, drawing his head carefully through the wire.

He moved one arm out and closed his fist around two links of the fence, then tightened his muscles so when he released the hand still on top of the fence, he could pull it out without touching a single razor.

On the other side, he hooked his feet into some links below him, stretched, grasped links at waist level, then let the weight of his body down on the strength of his arms.

When his feet touched the ground, a rush of heat went to his face and hope filled his heart. Usually, he went barefoot. It was quieter, and his toes were essential to climbing. You didn't want to negotiate a chase in shoes—not if you wanted to live. Here, though, he would leave on the sneakers they'd given him. This was rough ground.

The land sloped upward, although not steeply. It was fairly well wooded, which was a help to him, especially because all the lights in Willamette suddenly turned on and the bell started ringing.

He moved faster, heading for the top of the hill. He needed to get some idea of where he was. Behind him, he heard an engine start, then another, and in moments there were headlights moving through the woods, coming fast. Small trucks? No, four-wheelers, the kind the staff used.

A big voice: "Stop running, son. You can't get away!"

He would not stop.

From above, a huge light appeared, and with it the thunderous chopping roar of a helicopter. He'd watched helicopters from the roof of the Beresford. They were fascinating.

The helicopter's searchlight was playing along the edges of a nearby road, but he had no intention of going anywhere near a road. He continued to the top of the hill where, very suddenly, a view unfolded—even more magnificent than the one from the roof of the Beresford.

Keeping to the trees, listening to the clatter of the engines and the roar of the helicopter, he surveyed a gigantic ocean of lights. To the east, above the shadows of the mountains, the sky was a pink so perfect that it seemed to him in some way sacred.

Tears choked his throat. There was no time to waste, though. He headed down the far side of the hill, going toward houses that were buried in the trees.

He made progress, soon leaving his pursuers behind, at least for the moment.

There was a problem, though. He had no idea which way to go. In the Beresford, he could usually tell what floor he was on, no matter how dark it was or how fast he'd been moving. Outside, all was confusion, an incomprehensible complication of trees and streets full of madly rushing cars.

Moving more carefully, his tread so soft that he left only

the occasional track, he hopped a fence into a back garden. Here was a house with a swimming pool. The Beresford had a swimming pool, but he'd avoided it because of the cameras.

Time was passing, and what had been darkness when he left Willamette was now thin gray light. He looked around, seeking someplace to hide. He went toward a big house, but a dog started barking and, a moment later, lights began to turn on inside.

He hopped back over the fence and went to the next yard, and the one beyond it, and so on.

As he jumped a last fence, the helicopter suddenly popped up out of nowhere, so low that he could feel its prop wash on his back. Worse, the lights of the four-wheelers appeared, moving fast, heading straight for the row of houses.

He rushed along the side of the house, then out into the front yard. Crossing the street, he came to a ravine, which he leaped into immediately—and not a moment too soon. Police cars came screaming around the corners at either ends of the street. Policemen piled out and raced through yards, shining powerful flashlights into every bush and hiding place.

"Okay, son, we got you—come on outta there."

Except that they were pointing their flashlights at the wrong cluster of bushes.

Beresford went down the ravine, picking his way among the sharp stones, then moved up the side and into a more elaborate yard, this one with not only a pool but also a tennis court. Keeping between the fence that enclosed the court and the high brick wall that edged the property, he once again followed the side of the house, then slipped down the driveway and into the next street.

After a while, he could hear only the occasional distant *thutter* of the helicopter. He was fast and had gotten away.

He was soon passing storefronts, and there were people here and there on the quiet street. Farther along, there was a rattling sound as a merchant opened the front of his store.

Then he saw a police car. He stepped between two buildings, went down an alley, crossed a nearly empty parking lot, and came out on another street.

There was a bookstore in an old building. He went up to it, found a basement window, opened it with a few easy shakes, and slipped inside.

The dark was better. He felt a bit safer. But where was he now?

He crossed the cellar and opened a low door. Inside, there were dusty bottles of wine. He went in and pulled the door closed behind him. In the dark, he listened to his own breathing and tried to decide what to do.

CHAPTER 15

The Greek is roaring, every seat filled. You can hear the anticipation. Is my mouth gonna be too dry to sing?

Mom says, "Five minutes." She's hoarse from the ordeal of our final rehearsals.

I say, "Don't state the obvious." She nods. After the knock-down-drag-out over my beautiful boy, we've come to a silent agreement. She understands that I'm not some raving lunatic, and I accept her place as my mother and my manager. No more criticism, either side.

I think I have lost him. The juvie system is not telling us anything. I'm going to put the amazing feelings I have for him into my music.

The band is set up, the drums are riffing. Suddenly makeup people are all over me and I freak, but then my mike is in my hand and Timmy turns it on, and I know that every sound I now make will be heard by the crowd.

The stage is dark. My marks glow, the six step marks and the stop marks in night-glow tape. As I walk out, there is this awesome sense of bigness.

Silence. Then, with a *whoomp* of circuit breakers, the lights hit me, which feels like a physical slap of energy. We've lit rehearsals, of course, but not like this, not in the dark, and suddenly my entire body is glowing, my arms as if coated in white fire, the glitter of my blouse like stars around me, and my red boots two prancing flames as I take the mike to my lips and sing my very first hit, "I Want You." It's a girl just *saying it*, what they all want to hear, the long and the short of it, dammit, tell us, *tell us.*

"I want you, come with me, I want you, let me hold you, I want you, I want you. . . ."

I go on, but it doesn't click with them.

They are watching, waiting, and I feel this total horror, that all the controversy and media attention has built me into something bigger than I am, that Mom has filled this auditorium with more anticipation than I am worth.

They watch and I sing, and it feels like being torn to pieces with silence. I tell myself I am putting my heart into it, I caress my words, I cover them with my blood—"Don't leave me, I want you, I want you, don't tell me good-bye."

And they *watch*.

Agony. I want to be like a boxer who can go off and get pumped up for the next round. If I look into the wings, I can see Mom standing like a statue, Medea or Lady Macbeth, one of those tragic horrors, her face zombified by the steely reflected light from my funeral pyre.

The song ends and there is applause, but who wants *that*? I need screaming, I need total wild frantic mystical passion, or I am dead after tonight. That's the reality of music nowadays. Elvis or the Beatles could reach the entire world on one damn TV show. No more. I need ultimate buzz everywhere, or I am nothing.

Next, I do another of my hittish hits, "So Long, Boyfriend." This is slow and intimate, and it takes full advantage of the throaty whisper that haunts the edges of my voice. "Tomorrow I'm gonna meet you, tomorrow I'm gonna talk to you, tomorrow."

And they *watch*.

My heart beats harder, and I try harder, almost eating the microphone, willing myself to feel the longing that defines the song. "Tomorrow, I'm gonna love you, tomorrow I'm gonna hold you. . . ." A girl dreaming of a boy to whom she dares not speak. Alone in her room at night, knowing that this tomorrow will never come.

And now they do *not* watch. I think I can hear a new sound, a sort of low buzz, and I know what it is, under the band, under me. There is this sound coming up almost from my subconscious or whatever, but it's not coming from me; it's coming from them. They're talking. As I sing, they're *talking*, and I can feel them starting to tweet their disappointment to the world.

Why, why, why? I have no emotion left in me, nothing to transmit, nothing inside me but a heart so sad that it has turned to white winter ice, and snow queens cannot sing.

I do two more songs, and they might as well both be called the same thing—"Robot Girl." The more I lose them, the more shy I become, until I am practically whispering. You can hear the tears and the anger in my voice, and my throat is all tortured and dry, and I am barely even making a sound when suddenly—that's *HIM*! IT IS!

My heart has been a locked safe until this second, because right down there in the second row, looking up at me, is my beautiful boy with his wild blond hair and his huge shoulders.

Somehow he's escaped. Somehow he's come here.

I close the door of my soul on everyone except him. My eyes drill into his. My heart engages his heart, I can feel it. I cue my band and I go not to the next song in the set but rather to "Flying on Forever," which is the song of our tragedy and our hopes, and suddenly I am back out on the roof of the

Beresford in the night, looking out across the sea of lights to the low moon, and he is behind me, a reproachful sentinel.

"When you are remembered, you're not remembered at all, nobody's real, nobody falls, nobody at all . . . 'cause we're all flying on forever . . . forever . . . forever."

As I sing, conversations slow down, then finally stop. I stare straight at him, and he's noticed now. He looks back in confusion, and my heart practically tears itself into pieces when I realize that it's *not him*—it's some other boy who is wondering what's going on.

Oh, my poor lost boy, where are you? "Are you flying somewhere in the stars? Are you lost in the darkness of the lights? Are you flying . . . flying . . . flying?"

Then it's over. Silence fills the theater. I see a bat flutter through the lights and disappear.

Earthquake. Volcano. Never heard anything like it. Never knew such a sound could exist. A gigantic wave of noise, and the noise is clapping, it's yelling, it's foot-stomping. It's huge and totally awesome, and it makes me feel at once like dancing. And then they are coming toward me—the guy is actually coming up on the proscenium. I can see veins pulsating in his temples, his face is practically purple, his lips are twisted. He looks like some kind of monster.

Then he is at my feet and there are cameras flashing. Suddenly I'm jerked back, and I realize that guards are frantically pulling me away from him. My drummer, Mickey, and a guard are also pulling me, and for a second I think it *is* him! I lash out and scream at them and watch as he is swallowed up in the crowd. An instant later, about eight brown uniforms move off with him buried among them.

"I'm okay, man," the guy yells. "I'm okay," but they keep walking him out and then he is off somewhere in the crowd, gone.

Was it him, or wasn't it? I don't know, but my heart is just breaking now. Suddenly the drums start again and somebody puts my mike in my hand. The lights hit me.

The audience disappears into the blackness, and I yell back to the band, "So Not Free." I have no idea what we rehearsed—my mind is a blank. I have almost no idea even who I am, because I know now that what happened in that dark crawl space was way bigger than it felt at the time. It's burning me alive from the inside. I have to see him again.

I look out into the dark. Some longing part of my soul is looking back at me, and I feel this song as I have never felt any song before in my life. The words come out of me echoing with the loss of being a kid and looking at a future you thought would be free—the wonderful adult world that in reality is even less free than ours, and ours is *so not free.*

I sing not only from my heart and soul but from an even deeper place. I sing from behind the bars of life, but as I sing, I also see that the song is not entirely true—that all we have to do to find our freedom is to find love.

For a long moment, there is silence. Then a sound hits me. It's so loud that I think a bomb has gone off. Then I realize it's people clapping. They are clapping and yelling and stomping.

Somebody is yelling at me from the wings. Yelling at me to do something.

More. Yes, that's what they're yelling.

When I put the mike up to my lips, the whole audience turns off like a switch. I sing "Nature Boy."

At first, I sense a withdrawal from the crowd, as if they've been in the dark and are getting hit by light.

It happens again, though. Here I am singing this old song, and something opens up in me—a door, like, to another world.

The song ends. The applause comes again. The crowd surges forward, and I notice that a couple of the guards have their uniforms torn up, and there are cops—real ones—coming up on the stage and surrounding me.

As they lead me off into the wings, I say nothing. Being up there was incredible, and I know what it is now to be truly high, in the sense of being taken totally out of myself, of letting my heart flow like a river, of becoming something primitive and completely free.

Mom's face is covered in tears. She shakes so much it scares me. She looks suddenly little and old. I see that she is crying not only with joy for me but also with sorrow for herself.

This is her own life's dream, and now it has come true before her eyes, but it's not her.

When I embrace her, it does not feel like it always felt before, and I know exactly how it's different. She's not holding me. I am holding her.

When my mother grows old, this is how it will feel to cradle her in my arms, and I will do that. I will never turn away from her.

Then, as if she has read my thoughts, she leans back and looks me in the eyes. We both laugh and cry at the same time, me and my dangerous, evil, wonderful mom. Then Julius interrupts us. There is a police car waiting for us. We can't use the limo—the crowd is too hysterical.

I cannot express how weird this all makes me feel. You know they are putting you on a pedestal, but you still feel like yourself anyway.

So here we are in the back of a police car, and the cops are handing me programs for autographs for their kids. It's looking like I'm more of a guy thing than a girl thing, which is okay, I guess. Wonder who buys the most music?

I am a bit boy crazy, so it fits, I suppose. Interesting to be boy crazy while sealed up in the cocoon of fame. No boys in here, that's fer sure. Unless I want to be taken to a tea dance by some guy from, say, Megadeth, which I'm sure our publicists could arrange. Problem is, no celeb is going to date jailbait, and guys my own age are way too intimidated. I mean, who would invite me to a prom?

I have a tutor, hello? Is there a tutored-kids prom somewhere? Note to self—check that out.

We go into the Beresford by the back entrance, and the pig Frank is there. I'll get him, one way or another.

Back upstairs, the silence is kind of strange. You get used to applause real fast—and miss it just as fast.

I am sitting in the middle of my bed. I scoot up to the head of the bed and press my ear against the wall. It seems like just a minute ago I was being terrified by his breathing. But now it's totally quiet. Just the wall, nothing more.

I go out to the hall, heading for the den. From Mom's room, I hear music. And this is incredible: it's *my* music. She never just listens. It's always for work. Not tonight, though. She kissed me earlier. She had tears in her eyes.

Now she's shut up in there, and I'm wandering the halls, full of wishes that won't come true and desires that won't be fulfilled.

I go into the den and look at where his hatch used to be. Knowing Mom, the entire apartment is now encased in concealed armor plating.

He couldn't get in here, even if he *was* in the building.

I know he won't be coming out of juvie anytime soon. My one real way to get to him is to persuade Mom to hire a lawyer who can game the system for information.

Now that the concert has come and gone, maybe Mom will calm down, not only about my music but about life in general. She'll realize that she can't go bananas just because I like somebody.

Once we were transferred from the cop car to the limo, she put her head back and closed her eyes. Normally, she would have been all over me with critiques, checking things off on her clipboard, yelling into her BlackBerry, and sucking the plastic cigarette.

I leaned over and kissed her cheek, and a sort of rueful little smile came and went on her face. The rest of the way home, the car was quiet.

I go back to my room, lie down, and close my eyes.

Was it him in the audience, after all? Did I make a horrible mistake tonight?

No, he's lost deep in Willamette, or maybe somewhere else by now, even farther away. Could be anywhere.

Tomorrow is Sunday, but on Monday I'm going to ask our lawyers about him, and Mom is going to let me. She has no right to stand in my way.

I look at the clock—it's nearly three. I'm unbelievably tired but I'm also wired.

Safe in this big, strong building. Lonely. And so to sleep, perchance to dream of my poor lost boy.

CHAPTER 16

Frank arrived at Mr. Szatson's house gobbling Tums. Building the first device and then nearly getting caught had brought the whole situation home even more forcefully. If he did this, people were definitely going to die, and he was definitely going to be found out and given the needle.

He had no appointment and no idea how Mr. Szatson would react. But this was how it had to be.

As the ornate black gate swept open, he looked for signs of the guards he felt certain were there, but he saw nothing except the peaceful lawn and the flower beds.

He'd never considered himself a man with much of a conscience. What he had was a will to live, not a will to help others stay alive. But, dammit, didn't Szatson realize what he was doing? The investigation would be incredible. If they didn't both get caught, it would be a miracle.

He stopped his car in front of the house and got out, going up the steps to the big white front door. It was a formal house, red brick, that had once belonged to the chairman of some film studio. Probably to famous actors as well.

As he lifted his hand to ring the gleaming brass doorbell, the door swept open. Mrs. Szatson stood in front of him.

She smiled at him. "Luther?" she said softly, her voice a gentle lilt.

Szatson appeared behind her. "Good to see you again, Frank." He smiled. "Come on in." As they walked toward his office, he added, "Are you bringing a problem to our doorstep on a Sunday morning?"

"A little problem."

This time, there was the ghost of a reptile in Szatson's smile. "I don't handle little problems."

"It's not a little problem."

"I thought not."

Szatson crossed his big office and dropped into a chair. He gestured to Frank, but Frank remained in the doorway.

"Mr. Szatson, I don't think we can do this."

"Why?"

"Mr. Szatson, it's the crime of the century. It's going to be investigated beyond anything we've ever known. It's going to draw incredible, detailed, and prolonged attention to you."

"Frank, excuse me for being so blunt, but don't think ahead. That's my job, okay? So don't. Now, if you don't mind, my wife and I have to leave in five minutes."

He came over to Frank and put a friendly arm across his shoulder. "Frank, Frank, Frank . . ." He chuckled. "You're the smart one, so do the good job you've always done, you hear me?" Now he laughed. "Whatever will be will be, am I right?"

Not ten minutes after he'd arrived, Frank was back in his car. And what had he accomplished? Not a thing. It was still on. His warnings had been brushed off.

He drove around the corner and pulled over. He gripped the steering wheel, fighting for breath.

He couldn't do this, no way. But either way, he was a dead man. If he went through with it, he'd certainly be collared, imprisoned, and given a death sentence. Of course, Szatson would never allow him to walk away now—he knew too much. Szatson wouldn't just send him back to jail, either. He might even do it himself. But it would be done, no question. Frank would be dead, age thirty-two.

He drove back to the Beresford, passing the Beverly Hills Hotel and the restaurants and expensive boutiques along Sunset, then Amoeba Music and the ArcLight Cinema, where he sometimes went to the movies.

He turned into the parking garage, went down to his

space, and cut the engine. He started to get out, but instead he began shaking. A feeling came over him as if he was immersed in ice water, and the shaking became almost uncontrollable. He gripped the steering wheel, striking his head against it again and again.

Now that his attempt to scare Szatson off with warnings had failed, what was his next move?

He went into the building and headed through the employees-only door into the office zone. As he passed security, he tapped on the window, and Joe gave a wave of his fingers. Joe was happy with his little bit of money and watching his damn screens. Then he passed what had been the office of Renee Titer, who had been their rental agent back in the days when they did that.

Oh, how careful was this plan. The building was even designed for fire values, the structure coming in just this side of codes—except for that shaft extension, of course. That was the key to the whole plan, as it had been from the first.

From the first. That was the amazing evil of it. True evil. Satanic evil.

He reached his office, standing for a moment and looking at the black door with the sign on it that said, simply, SUPERINTENDENT. Then he went in and sat down. For a time, he stared into space. He opened his desk.

The new detonator he had built was black because he had covered it with electrical tape. It was about the size of a box of matches. He took it in his hand. It was feather-light and so simple. Its job was to ignite a tungsten filament. But this would happen deep in one of the fuel tanks, inside the oil.

He cradled it. He felt the weight of the building above him, and in his mind's eye he saw the people in the apartments above, some sleeping, some watching TV, some just getting up late on a Sunday morning, others making love perhaps, whatever. He thought of the little singer way up there where there would be no escape. That death alone would make this fire famous.

He laid the detonator on his desk and looked at it under the hard fluorescent light. He could smell the faint odor of the electrical tape. Why had he covered it with tape? He'd wanted it to survive, somehow. But why? It would not survive, not any part of it.

He peeled back some of the tape. The electronics were simple. He had put them together in ten minutes—a twelve-volt battery, a small timer, a piece of tungsten. He'd designed it himself, and he knew it would be effective.

His fingers seemed huge in comparison with the small timer he'd bought at Target. He pressed the Set button. It began counting back from thirty minutes. Half an hour to the worst disaster in Los Angeles since the Northridge Earthquake.

He would drop it in tank two, the center of the three tanks, then he would tell Joe he was leaving, and he would go down to the IHOP on Olympic and eat pancakes until he heard the sirens.

Briefly, he thought he might just go ahead and kill himself. But he knew he was too much of a coward to do it.

Twenty-seven minutes. He touched the box. It was a strange thing to contemplate what it would mean to this building and its occupants, to the city and the world, if he closed it and took it down the hall.

He watched the timer count down until it reached the twenty-five-minute mark.

Making sure nobody was in the hall, he left his office. As he walked down the corridor with the device, he found that he had to wipe away tears. But he didn't feel sad, at least not in any part of his heart that he was in touch with.

"Hey there, Frank."

"Hi, Joe, where'd you come from?"

In answer, Joe glanced toward the men's room down the hall. Then he returned to the security office. Frank went on. He didn't think that Joe had the slightest chance of survival so he couldn't even look at him. He reached the end of the hall and climbed down the spiral stairs that led to the main equipment floor, where the steam generators were housed, along with the backup electrical generators.

He didn't see the figure that appeared in the hallway behind him, slipping out of a storage closet. Luther Szatson watched him carefully as he disappeared down the spiral stairs.

Luther had been hard at work on this for a long time, and Frank Turner was going to take the entire hit for the catastrophe.

Clear and simple, Frank had been set up. Even while he was still in prison, the frame was built around him. He'd been chosen carefully. First, he'd done good work in the past. Second, he could be blackmailed because he'd been released illegally.

Szatson went past the security office with its big window. He stuck his head in the door. "Joey, where's Frank?"

Joe glanced at his monitors. "Don't see him. Want me to give him a call?"

"Yeah, do that."

Joe picked up his walkie-talkie. "Hey, Frank, Mr. Szatson's here." He waited. "Come in, Frank." He waited longer, then repeated the message.

As Luther knew perfectly well, the walkie-talkie's signal wasn't going to penetrate into the fuel storage area, blocked as it was by the big iron of the generators above.

"I saw him heading toward mechanicals, but he's not in there now."

"I'll go take a look," Luther said. "If he turns up, please ask him to wait for me in his office."

"Is anything the matter, Mr. Szatson?"

"Nothing that can't be handled."

Luther then went down to the end of the hall and opened

the fire door into the machine room. It was almost silent, with only one steam generator running, emitting nothing more than a soft whine.

Moving carefully so that his heels wouldn't clatter on the grating of the floor and alert Frank, he went to the steel hatch that led down into the fuel storage area. Below, the lights were on. Frank was up on a ladder, bending over the middle of the three huge fuel tanks.

Very quietly, Luther lifted the hatch and put it down over the opening. He then slid the locking bar in place with his foot. He would later say that he had done it because there had appeared to be nobody in the fuel storage area and it was a code violation for it to be open.

He went back to the security office. "Not there," he told Joe.

"That's funny, because I didn't see him come back. You looked down below?"

"It's closed."

Joe thought for a moment. "You can't close it from inside, so he must've gone out while I was . . . I don't know—I had my back turned."

"You're not required to be monitoring this hall, so it's no skin."

"I just like to notice. I like to be aware." Joe stood up. His break time had arrived. "I'm taking my break, Mr. Szatson."

"Sure thing."

So Joe went upstairs, without the slightest idea that, by doing so, he was saving his own life.

In the fuel storage room, Frank was working up a sweat as he methodically unscrewed the big bolts that kept one of the inspection ports sealed. You could see through the ports, but the tanks were not intended to be opened unless absolutely necessary.

Grunting, pushing against the long handle of the wrench, he finally got the last bolt to move. As he opened the inspection port, fumes from the warm furnace heating oil filled his nose, choking him and making his eyes water. The oil had to be kept at a constant hundred degrees, or it would be too thick to flow through the system. This was no home heating system on a larger scale. It was completely different and far more complicated.

Now was the moment. He had laid the box atop the fuel tank. He picked it up and opened it. Just eleven minutes left. But that was good—it was enough time to get well out of the basement area before the explosion. He did not think anyone down here was going to survive for even a second.

The fire would travel up the building's various chases and shafts, then blossom when it reached the top of the building. The top three floors would start burning immediately. Lower down, the process would be slower. To an unknown extent, the building's sprinkler system would retard the flames. But in an explosion like this, standpipes would be wrecked up and down the line, and there was no way to tell how many of the sprinklers would work, or for how long. If Szatson had done his construction right, they wouldn't work for very long at all.

He closed the small firebomb, then immersed the detonator in the oil. Circulators inside the tank kept the oil in motion, and the box soon disappeared into the thick blackness.

It was done. And he did not feel anything—except, of course, urgency. He had to get out now. He could not waste time, but even as quick as he was, by the time he was going up the spiral stairs again, he had only nine minutes left.

The hatch was closed.

He looked at it. How could this be?

Then his heart *really* started hammering. "Hey, Joe! Joey! You locked me in, dammit! JOEY!"

The moron had found the hatch open and closed it. What did they give him, a monkey brain? Obviously, if it was open, somebody was in here. With shaking hands, he pulled his walkie-talkie off his belt. The damn thing had better work because eight minutes might not be enough time to get this open from the inside.

"Joey, you locked me in the oil hole!"

Static.

"Joey!"

Static.

Too much steel. It had never worked in here, and it never

would. But hell, Joe would have at least called down. Nobody in his right mind would close this hatch without checking the space. The lights were still on. Joe wouldn't close the hatch and leave them on. He would definitely have turned them off, which would have alerted Frank immediately.

The truth hit him. *This was not an accident.*

Of course not—how stupid had he been! Szatson would never, ever let a man with knowledge like he had live.

Szatson had done it.

Frantic now, he leaped down the stairs, grabbed the ladder, and threw it against the oil tank. He pulled off the hatch cover and peered in, but saw only slowly roiling blackness. Even if the box came to the surface, he would never find the incendiary sunken in all that oil.

Maybe he could drain the tank, then close the valve so that nothing would explode but fumes and residual oil.

Dropping down, he looked for some sort of emergency release valve, but there wasn't one. He could see where the piping went out to the fuel oil fill station behind the building, but there was nothing anywhere that would release oil into the room itself. Maybe it was possible to drain it into the sewer. Surely the tanks had to be cleaned.

No, they didn't. This was modern equipment that didn't build up residue. It never needed cleaning.

Four minutes. Almost dizzy with fear, he took a wrench

up to the hatch and began hammering on it with all his strength.

"Damn you, Joey, WAKE UP!" *WHAM, WHAM, WHAM.*

Fire. It would hurt, it would be agony, and it was death, the real thing, *death*—and why had he done it? He hadn't wanted to. He had tried to talk Szatson out of it.

"God! God, it's wrong, I know it's wrong!" *WHAM, WHAM, WHAM.*

Two minutes.

Hissing. What was it? No, it was early, *it was early.*

Fire was gushing out of the inspection port. The hissing became a roar.

His whole body, all at once, felt as if his skin was being ripped off.

Fire.

Chapter 17

Beresford's muscles were screaming, his head was pounding, his lungs sucking agonized breaths. He had been running for hours, always moving in the direction of the tall buildings he glimpsed occasionally. He'd tried to stop cars, but nobody would let him in. When he'd seen police cars, he'd gone the other way or hidden.

He took big, ragged strides down the shoulder of a highway with cars speeding past just inches from him. To his left was the wall that enclosed the highway; above it appeared the sheer facade of the Beresford. A sunken highway ran along the west side of the building. You could see it when you looked down.

Ahead was an exit ramp, but it was narrow and had no shoulder. Nonetheless, he had to get up there, so he took it, squeezing himself as tightly as he could against the concrete wall. The cars passed him so close that some of them actually bumped against his right thigh. There was honking, the squeal of brakes, shouting.

Then he was high enough to reach the top of the wall, and with his great arm strength, he hoisted himself up.

Before him stood the side wall of the Beresford, its cladding gleaming black in the soft midmorning light. Ahead was the front of the building, with its doorman and concierge and other lobby personnel. He must not go near them; he must not let them see him.

Quickly, he trotted across the street and went down the alley behind the building. There was no concealed way to enter except that one door. In the front there would be more building personnel, and he feared that he wouldn't have time to explain the situation before they called the police.

He had to get into the fuel storage area and get that bomb out of there. Again and again, he'd tried to think who would put it there. Terrorists was the only answer he could think of, but how had they gotten into the depths of the building like that?

He came out the far end of the alley. Now he was on the east side of the building, and the entrance to the parking garage was just ahead. It was not attended, so the only chance he had of being seen was if somebody happened to be driving out and became suspicious.

As he hurried toward the parking level elevator lobby, he thought of only two things: the bomb in the basement and Melody on the top floor. In the back of his mind, though, were less formed thoughts of all the other people in the building, and all the animals, and the fact that the explosion would be so dangerous.

A few more steps and he would be standing in front of the elevators. But he did not take those steps, because he also knew that he would then be on camera.

To one side of the four elevators was an alarmed entrance to the emergency stairs, and if he opened that door, not only would an alarm sound, another one would go off in the security office. He wouldn't get two flights before he was caught.

But he had a better way. One of the chases came all the way down to this level. From this side, its opening was buried behind the spray-on ceiling material. But Beresford knew that it was like all the other chases—open-shaft construction.

To reach it, he stood on the hood of a car and pushed at the ceiling material until he found an area that had give. Then he pushed a fist through and tore at the ceiling until he had made a hole large enough to enter.

The car he was standing on was now a mess, but that didn't matter. From here, it would take him just a couple of minutes to reach the crawl space between the two basements. He would remove a few ceiling tiles and drop right down into the machine room, then make his way to the fuel storage area.

This was the same shaft he used to reach Melody, and being in it again made him think of her fifty stories above him. Right now, he could only hope that she was safely away from the building. But why would she be on the morning after her big concert? She'd be resting.

He looked up into the darkness. There was a faint light that he knew came from the elevator shaft—again, an open shaft that should have been closed.

How he longed to just climb to Melody and get her out of here—and Mom, too, even Mom. Because he knew that Melody loved her, despite all their fights. So he loved Mom. Not like his own mother, of course, but he would fight for her life if he had to, no question there.

The second he got the bomb out of the building, he would tell Melody and Mom everything, and he was going to make them stay out of the building until the police had searched every inch of it.

He was just raising himself into the chase when there came a distant sound, a pop like bacon frying, but louder. The chase was lit yellow, and he dropped down onto the car and rolled away as a big ball of fire burst out of the hole.

For a second, he was too shocked to move. The chase was

now filled with flickering light. He raised his head into fume-choked heat. If that fireball had hit him, he would be dead.

He looked up. The higher reaches of the chase were still untouched.

He had to climb, and he had to do all fifty stories or Melody was going to die. He pulled himself up into the chase. Off at the end of the crawl space there was roiling fire, but it was boiling up the elevator shaft and the chase that ended in the equipment room, not this one. This one would be clear for a while.

Without another thought, he started up, climbing hand over hand, pulling himself on pipes, doing it the way he had always known. Except, this time there was a difference. This time he was already terribly tired, and as he grabbed pipe and drew himself up, he felt unaccustomed pain in his muscles.

Still, he continued. Normally, he could do twenty stories with ease, thirty if he really wanted to push it. Then he'd rest for a couple of minutes and go on. There was no time for that now, and he forced his body to keep working, forced himself to ignore the torment in his muscles and the fire in his lungs.

Then, as he passed forty, he heard barking and immediately recognized Gilford's voice. He cried out in anguish. He couldn't let Gilford die in a fire! But Melody—she was in bigger trouble way up there.

Moving as fast as he could, he went to Tommy's and dropped down.

"Hello! Anybody home?"

Only Gilford, who jumped up and down, snorting happily. The apartment was filled with a haze of smoke, and the detectors were buzzing.

He picked the wiggling dog up, went to the front door, and opened it. He already knew that this was safe; he'd seen from the crawl space that there was no fire here yet.

He could hear others crying out, and he ran up and down the hall, hammering on doors.

"Get out! Use the front fire stairs!" he shouted. They would be safe, at least for a while. He assumed that the pressure of the explosion would have blown in the doors on the back stairs, at least up to the lobby. So they were likely full of smoke, probably fire, too.

He ushered people toward the stairs, giving Gilford to a woman he didn't know and making sure that Cheops, the Egyptian cat from 4033, and Modred, Sam and Angela Parker's big old Lab, were also safe.

Then he returned to Tommy's apartment and reentered the crawl space, continuing on his journey upward. As he passed forty-one, he saw elevator four stuck at an angle, smoke pouring up around it. From inside he heard terrible, terrible screaming.

He could not pass. He had to go over there. So he jumped the chase and headed for the smoke- and flame-filled elevator shaft.

He got to the elevator, which was shaking, and he could hear coughing and crying. Jumping onto the roof of the elevator car, he started choking, too, because the smoke was thick here. Just above him was the pull-down lever that opened the shaft to the fiftieth floor, but he was not going to pull it because it would only increase the draft, drawing the fire up from below even faster.

The cars had access hatches in their ceilings, but they weren't really for escape. They were maintenance shafts, and narrow. He unhooked the four latches and pulled the cover off, pushing it away past the cable housing. Faintly, it went clattering away into the glow from below, which was rapidly increasing.

Inside the elevator, there were two people. One of them was Mrs. Scutter.

Her face was black, her hair partly burned, and she was shaking so badly that, when he dropped down into the car, he could barely lift her birdlike frame onto its roof.

There was a man there, also, and Beresford was horrified to see that his skin was raw and broken, his clothes almost burned off. This man was standing, looking down at himself, muttering.

"Come on," Beresford said. "We're getting out of here."

Then he recognized this man. It was Luther.

His burns were terrible, but Beresford could only hate his father's murderer. Had he been in the basement? He must have been. Beresford lifted him onto the top of the car, then he came out of the thick, overheated air only to find that the smoke around the car was practically impenetrable.

There was no fire control system in this shaft, and the flames already seemed close to maybe the eighth floor. Dropping down from above were molten bits of plastic burning off pipes and wire sheathing on the top two floors. The fireball that had come up this shaft and the north chase had set the underroof on fire, and flames were now spreading there. The fiftieth floor would be trapped, and roof access was probably already impossible.

Time was rushing by. He had stopped to rescue others, and now he feared there might be no way to get Melody and her mother out.

Dragging a shrieking Mrs. Scutter, he crossed the crawl space to the south chase, then moved a few feet until he was above one of his hatches. He threw it open and lowered her into the apartment. "Go feel the door. If it's hot, don't open it. If it isn't, go to the front fire stairs. Do you understand?" When she nodded, wide-eyed, he left her.

Then he went back to Luther, but it was too late. He looked into the faded eyes, at the surprise and shock that still haunted them. Poor man, he thought. But ironic, too, that the person responsible for all the violations would also be killed because of them.

The other elevators were far down at the bottom of the shaft, enveloped in flames. He could only hope that nobody had been in them.

The chase was getting hot now and filling up with fumes. Even so, he returned and began going up once again, forcing himself not to waste breath by uselessly screaming her name.

The building shook, and suddenly he was casting a long shadow ahead. He didn't need to be told what this meant—he threw himself into the crawl space between forty-two and forty-three just as a solid wall of flame came up from below and filled the chase.

He screamed then, not because he had been burned—he hadn't—but because this meant only one thing. Melody was now hopelessly trapped.

CHAPTER 18

I don't know what it is, but it smells *horrible* and there are bells ringing and I hear sirens and—*Mommy, the ceiling has smoke, the ceiling has smoke.*

It's impossible; it has to be some kind of weird nightmare. I feel like I'm in mud or something, like I can't move. From the hall, I hear terrible screaming, again and again and again, screaming and banging against the walls.

I try 911 on my cell, but it won't work.

"Mom! Mom!" I go out into the living room, and she is there, bent over the phone. The front of her hair is all curled and black, and the whole place stinks of burned hair. She looks up at me, and it's as if we are both dreaming as she says, "I can't get this to work," and hands me the phone.

This is not happening. It cannot be happening. I see that her bedroom door is shut and there is a sort of haze by the door, and under the door is flickering light.

This phone is dead. I curse at it, and she bursts into tears.

I have to get out of here. I cannot bear this, not one second longer. I run for the front door and grab the handle—it's as hot as an iron! I scream, and Mom screams, "DON'T OPEN THAT!"

She grabs me from behind, drags me away by my hair—*my hair, that's right*—growling like a tiger, and, my God, she looks like a creature from another planet with big, bulging eyes and a face as gray as somebody already dead.

"Mom, here—" I run into my room and grab my computer and open it. It comes to life, so I call up the Internet, and *it works.*

"I'm online!"

I go to Twitter and tweet "Help we are burning Apt 5050 Beresford Melody McGrath Call 911 Help we are burning call 911 call call call 911!"

I press Update, and it just sits there going, "Loading." *Loading,* oh, God, it's not posting. I watch. It will not post! Come on, COME ON! But it will not post.

Then I realize the truth. That was a cached page. I'm not online at all.

As a helicopter passes the windows, I glimpse the pilots, their faces turned toward the building.

"Mom!" I run and grab my bedspread. The ceiling is now all cracked, and smoke is sort of shooting down in puffs, like people on the other side are blowing cigarette smoke through little holes.

"Help me!" I go back to the living room and start to open the door onto the balcony, but Mom grabs my wrist.

"No."

"No? There's a helicopter right there!"

"If we open that door, we'll create a draft." She says it quietly, as offhandedly as a teacher explaining a problem she has explained many times before. Then she covers her face with her hands and begins shaking. But then she stops.

"Mom?"

A great cry comes out of her, and she throws her head back with her fists to her temples and howls. I scream, too. I scream because she is screaming, and I know it's because we are going to burn and there's nothing we can do and nobody can save us.

The smell is horrible, and oh, God, I am so afraid. I am so afraid that I am just about to burn. I'm going on the balcony, and I am going to jump. If the fire comes near me, I will. I will!

Again, the helicopter passes. But what can they do? How can they help us?

Smoke is coming out of my room, so I pull the door closed. That is my life in there: my dolls, my snuggly Boo-Boo that my daddy gave me when I was four, my iPad, and, oh, God, the one thing I cannot lose, my guitar.

All of a sudden, a strange sort of calm comes over me. I am going to die, and I am going to either see God or be nothing. My mind starts saying it over and over—"see God or be nothing, see God or be nothing"—and that seems to make it all real and unreal at the same time.

"Mom," I say as I return to the living room, "MOM! MOM! MOM!"

She comes out of the kitchen. We throw our arms around each other.

The water stopped working almost right away, so she was gathering up all the Cokes and stuff and soaking kitchen towels with them.

"Help me," she says.

We line them up at the bottom of the front door. The door is so hot that the towels hiss when they touch it. The hall must be a complete firestorm, and that door is liable to blow open at any minute. In fact, Mom was right about not going out on the balcony. If we slide that door open, the smoke and fire will blow into the foyer and the apartment will become an inferno.

Again, I hear sirens. They seem miles away.

Mom grabs my shoulders. "They're coming," she says. She

laughs and her face is scary. "They'll be right up." Solid confidence in her voice.

No, they won't. I know what happens to skyscrapers when they catch fire. Everybody does.

I nod to Mom. She kisses me, covers my face with kisses.

"My baby, my baby," she says, and I see over her shoulder that one of the towels we just put against the door is smoking, and then I see a slim tongue of flame rise along it, leaving a dark scar where it licks against the door.

I run into the kitchen and open the freezer, and there are still ice cubes in the icemaker. I pull out the whole thing and go back and throw ice against the flame.

The flame goes down, but the ice hisses into steam when it touches the door. I realize that our time is almost up—we must only have minutes. And no sooner do I think this than the flame comes back, and another one beside it, low, flickering.

Then there is another sound—*pop pop . . . pop . . . poppop*. It's Mom's bedroom door now. Her room must be full of fire, and the hollow wood door is not going to last much longer.

"Mom, we have to try to escape."

"Don't open the front door! Don't touch it!"

"There's that crawl space I was in, remember that?"

"Oh, that's got to be a deathtrap."

"We could break through the den closet. We could, I know it!"

She points upward. The ceiling is full of little cracks, and more of them are appearing by the second. I realize that the crawl space above it must be filled with fire. The ceiling will fall any second and I am going to catch on fire then, and it hits me all over again, the idea of burning and feeling that pain. I look again at the glass wall and the big doors and the balcony on the other side.

The sky has dozens of helicopters, some close, some farther away, all of them, I know, with cameras on this building.

"WHY DON'T THEY SAVE US?"

Mom has Perrier water, which she opens and pours over me. She cries as she does it, then she takes me in her arms and encloses me in herself as best she can. Long, deep red tendrils cross the ceiling.

"We have to try the balcony."

"Don't open doors and windows during a fire. Close all doors and windows."

"Mom, it doesn't matter anymore. Either we stay here and burn or we take our chances out there. A little more time, Mom! And maybe that's all we need. Maybe all we need is a little more time, and they'll get to us."

"If we open that door, it's over, honey."

"What if they don't know we're even here? What if they think the apartment is empty?"

To get some attention we hang her bright red robe on the

curtain rods, and when I get up on the couch, the air is so hot it hurts my head.

I decide that I will not burn. I will not let the fire destroy my face. I will jump instead. But I am so afraid of heights.

And yet I stood on the edge barely a week ago! How stupid that seems now. How incredibly, totally stupid and self-centered. Poor little rich girl.

Right here and now, I pledge that if I survive this I will become a better person. I go to my knees.

"God, if I live, I will change my life."

Mom comes down beside me, kneeling also, and she bows her head. "Forgive me, Lord. I tried so hard, and I made mistakes." She sobs, tries to say more, and can't.

"We did it together," I say to her.

We hug each other, and I think what I bet she is thinking, too, that ambition can make you great or it can make you evil, and if we get out of this, we are both going to change. We'll use our ambition and my celebrity to do worthwhile things.

There is the chugging of a helicopter again, and we both hold out our arms, begging for rescue.

There is a sling under the chopper and a woman in it. We can see her face clearly.

They have rescued our neighbor in 5052.

"HELP US," Mom shouts, "OVER HERE!" Then her voice breaks. "Oh, God, they can't see us!"

"We have to risk it," I say. I go toward the doors.

"NO!"

The voice that comes out of me is almost primal, it's so big and furious and powerful. "WE WILL RISK IT!"

She closes her eyes. We both know our situation. Die here because nobody can see us, or go out on the balcony and risk burning to death or having to jump.

For a second, I feel this other person inside me, and I discover a truth about myself—I am what I am at sixteen because I am no innocent little girl. I might be a kid, but I have power, and I feel it now.

Mom pulls open the door to the balcony and we run out, but before we can close it, there is a ferocious wind and the whole inside of the apartment fills up with flame.

She shuts the door, but the glass starts crazing as flames boil against it.

There is no time, I know that now, there is *no* time! I run to the edge, she runs to the edge, and we lean over because there is smoke behind us—if we do not lean out, we will suffocate. It's hot, it hurts, and it's getting hotter fast.

A helicopter appears. It thunders, bounces in the air fifty feet away, and comes closer—but suddenly the fire blows it back away from us. Then another one comes, higher up, and I can see a long hose dangling from it. It hovers in the smoke overhead, and there is gushing water, and I feel the coolness of the spray.

But it misses! Most of it just goes down past us and into the street!

Mom screams. She holds out her hands, begging, and then something else—a sling—comes down out of the smoke. It is orange, attached to a rope.

Mom grabs it and comes toward me, but at that same moment the rope tightens and *she is pulled off the balcony and into the air.*

She doesn't have it on. She's going to fall. Mom, *Mom*!

She disappears upward into the smoke, still clinging to it.

I drop down to the tile floor, where I used to dance, where I was supposed to prance around in that robe for the papis in another world, on another planet, in a distant age. I can't watch Mom's body fall. I will never forget the look on her face as she swung out, her eyes so full of pain and terror.

But here comes the sling again! Did they save her? Is she alive? Did she not fall?

"Mommy!"

The sling bobs, sways, and comes closer, closer still! I reach for it, but it swings away. I reach for it, grasp it—yes! I grasp it and pull it toward me, but there is a low, hungry sound, almost as if the fire has a voice, and that voice is saying "noooo." There is *searing heat*, and I throw myself to the tiles as the entire glass wall disintegrates. I am lying seven feet from the glaring, flaming maw of the blast furnace that our apartment has become.

And the sling—*the sling is a molten blob of burning plastic.*

It disappears into the smoke.

Now it's quiet. I am alone, me and the fire and God. "Please don't mind if I jump, God, please don't mind because I don't want to burn, and I am, oh, God—*I am burning—ow—ow—*"

Then—what?—hands on the balcony, hands coming up. On the edge, somebody is coming over somehow, but from where? It's impossible.

And then I see his blond hair and his big, pale eyes and his huge muscles, and I realize that it's HIM! Jesus—it's my beautiful boy! Oh my God, he's trapped, too.

He slithers across the railing and down, staying under the smoke and fire that are boiling out of the apartment. He lies on me, and instantly it's cool. His shirt and pants are soaked with sweat.

"Now, listen," he says. "I am going to carry you. I want you to close your eyes, love."

"Yes, I will close my eyes."

"It's going to be very hard, and we might fall."

"Yes, love."

His arms come around me. I realize that he is breathing really hard, grunting.

He lifts me into sudden heat, terrible heat, but I force back my screams. All I can think is that my magic boy is here, and

I wonder, is this a dream given to me by God? Am I really burning right now?

I am under one of his arms, and he is carrying me like a bag of potatoes; he is lifting me. It's getting cooler.

He told me to keep my eyes closed, but I do not do that.

I open them.

At first I don't understand what I am seeing—a long, gleaming black cliff disappears into the hazy distance.

Then I see movement, and I realize that all those red things are fire trucks, their lights flashing, and those white pillars are streams of water hitting the lower floors of the building. There are also TV vans down there, dozens of them.

He is carrying me down the side of the building. And he's having trouble; I can hear him gasping, and I feel us—oh, God—I feel us starting to slip.

Then, no, we go another floor, and I see how he's doing it with the tips of the fingers of one hand, then with his toes, climbing the ribbing between the panels that make up the side of the building.

We will fall. I close my eyes and pray, "God, give him a chance. He is so young. He hasn't had much in his life, please. . . ."

We slip and he cries out, but somehow he gets us steady again. I hear helicopters everywhere. Another rescue sling comes down, but then it goes away. We can't get to it.

It's terrible to be in this, but he is so strong—his arm around me is beyond steel. I love this boy with all my heart. I want him to be rescued, to be saved—I want this with all that I am.

He stops. He is breathing hard. His muscles are like marble, hard and suddenly cold. Sweat pours out all over him. I open my eyes. I see the side of his head and his other arm, his fingers clinging to the wall ... and his fingers are *purple*.

When he lets go, we die. I close my eyes again, trying to be as still as possible, to imagine myself as light as a feather, as light as air. I think, the first guy who ever loved me died for it, and I just want to bawl. It's so unfair to him, it is *so unfair*.

Now we are moving again. Incredibly, he is bending his legs, going down another floor somehow. Oh, it's impossible, it must be—and then we slip. . . .

We are falling. The wind is screaming and I am screaming. Time has stopped, and I see in his face total love. Looking at me. Total love.

Then *wham*. Black. *Thud*.

We are lying side by side in a rescue net. There are faces all around us, staring. Men in helmets.

Suddenly I understand: he got us close enough to the ground to drop into a net.

We're alive!

"Don't move, now. We're just putting the net down—don't move. Let EMS come to you."

A moment later, I feel a hardness come up under me, and the men stand up. They are tall, like sentinels in their black coats.

Then a woman in an orange smock bends over me.

"Do you hurt anywhere, honey?"

"I ... my hand ... I burned my hand."

They lift me and put me on what feels like the most comfortable bed in the world. It starts moving, and I see above me the gigantic, towering side of the Beresford with a massive plume of smoke above it. Helicopters are circling, dropping water loads onto the roof, which seems to be where most of the fire is.

There's a thunder of engines all around me as countless fire trucks pump water into the shattered lower floors. I'm rolled under the building marquee, and he's beside me, also on a gurney, and then suddenly I'm wheeled away. I cry out for him.

There are dozens of people from the fire in the hospital. A woman looks down at me. Her face is covered with soot, her hair is burned into little melted knots, but her eyes are swimming in silent tears.

"Mel? Mel, honey?"

"MOM!"

We touch, our hands grasping. There's so much between the two of us.

Then, like a flash, she's gone and I am no longer in a

hallway. I am in a room. Time passed. How much time, I don't know.

I try to figure it out, but I keep drifting away. Am I drugged? Yeah, there's an IV . . . plastic gleaming in the light. Am I burned? My face? No . . . hand. I remember, my hand was burned.

The TV is on. There is a video playing.

Mom's voice: "That's you, honey, you and Beresford."

Beresford? *Beresford*? "Mom, what—where—"

"It's the most incredible rescue ever recorded. He carried you forty-five stories down the side of the building. Nobody knows how he did it."

"Beresford! BERESFORD!"

"Sleep now . . . sleep."

"No! I want him! Where is he?"

They are silent. I see a nurse's long hand move toward my IV. And I feel sleepy, but I don't want to sleep. I must see him now!

"He's not dead—he can't be!"

Screaming. I hear terrible screaming. I don't want to hear it. I try to cover my ears and scream back.

Hands touch my face, powerful hands. I realize that it's me doing all the screaming, and I fight for control—and then there are lips against my mouth, lips covering my screams.

Deep breaths, one after the other. I feel long hair drifting along my cheeks. I see his face, those big, wonderful eyes. Oh my God, he is alive!

I cry harder than I have ever cried in my life as Beresford wraps his big arms around me. I just sink into his amazing strength, so happy to be alive and with him. It seems like a miracle that we're both still part of the world, and Mom, too. I hear music in my soul.

He isn't there long, though, and I can't tell if he's leaving on his own or being taken away; there are so many people in here. I see uniforms and scream after him, but he's gone just like that, absorbed in the riot.

A warm feeling spreads through me, and I shout, "No, NO," but I can't fight it. It's total peace, and I know they have hit me with a knockout punch of some sort of sedation.

But my heart keeps screaming, screaming for him.

Then I'm floating. I don't want to float, but I just can't stop myself. He disappears into a cloud of sleep, and I fear that this time, for sure, he's gone forever.

Epilogue

More people watched the blurry figure crawling slowly down the side of the burning building than watched the first landing on the moon. As Beresford's impossible struggle unfolded, an entire world stopped and looked to their TVs at home, in bars, in store windows, on planes, everywhere there was television. And then came the last, perilous jump, the boy and girl like two rag dolls flopping out of the sheets of smoke and onto the huge inflatable cushion the firefighters had deployed.

"They're being rushed to the hospital. Nobody knows their condition."

Everyone waited, millions upon millions of people from Los Angeles to London to Tokyo.

The director of emergency services at Downtown Receiving Hospital came to read a statement.

"One hundred and fifty-three emergency cases have been accepted at this hospital from a structural fire at the Beresford Downtown Apartments. We have eighty patients in critical condition with burns, and they are being relocated to hospitals throughout the region."

Reporters yelled about Melody and the boy, but the doctor still didn't have any information.

It turned into a siege, with cameras, reporters, news anchors, bloggers, and columnists all waiting for the answer.

Finally, the doctors were sure of themselves. Melody McGrath and the unidentified young man who had rescued her were alive but in critical condition. Melody had a broken leg, a burned hand, and internal injuries, and the unidentified young man had second-degree burns, was suffering from smoke inhalation, and had a dislocated shoulder.

Beresford was in a charity ward with five other homeless patients. Each day, he got a little better.

Melody drifted in and out of consciousness. She was aware of pain, then of painlessness, then of a deep loneliness that filled her eyes with tears.

She struggled with infection and a heart murmur, and three days after the fire, the doctors told her mother that she had a cardiac infection.

Her mom stayed with her day and night, sleeping in a

chair, listening to the heart monitor, praying and worrying and resolving again and again to repair her relationship with her daughter.

Her dad came and made a promise to be in her life more, and she hoped it was true.

Down in the charity ward, there came a day when two caseworkers from Social Services arrived, and Beresford was released into their custody.

Eleven days after she had been admitted, Melody found herself staring at what at first she thought was a fog bank, but then realized was a ceiling.

Was there smoke? What was happening?

"Honey?"

"Beresford. Please, Mom, where is he?"

Hilda was embarrassed because she had been so concerned about Melody's state that she hadn't thought about him for days. When she finally called patient services, she was told that he had recovered. "He's fine," she said. "I'm sure he'll come see you when he can."

"Where is he?"

"He's in a group home."

Melody was heartbroken, a devastated angel lying in her ever-changing sea of flowers, hollow-eyed and silent.

"You did this, didn't you?"

"What?"

"You got rid of him. You had him sent away. Oh, Mom, where is he? I need him!"

"I didn't. I didn't do—" And now Hilda realized her mistake. She hadn't done anything. She'd just let Beresford get sucked up in the system.

She had often been outraged at this complicated, talented daughter of hers. But now, and perhaps for the first time, she was outraged at herself. Ashamed, really.

"I'll find him. I'll bring him back to you, Mel."

In these terrible weeks watching her daughter hover between life and death, Hilda Cholworth learned a lot of things, about love and how it must give—and also forgive. She had seen Mel glow when Beresford came in the room, a joy that she herself had never known.

Social Services had just been doing its job. They had no idea that they had inspired an attack from a one-woman army.

Hilda learned about the fostering process. She hired a lawyer, fired him, hired another. She went before judges, shuffled papers, signed documents, sucked her plastic cigarette, and worked far into the night in her cluttered hotel room near the hospital. No matter what it took, she intended to fulfill her promise to Mel.

It turned out that Beresford was in a group home in Westlake. He wasn't a prisoner, not exactly, but he wasn't free to come and go, either. She talked to the manager of the home, who e-mailed her the house rules. She bit her cigarette to pieces and fumed.

Then she found a new judge, who was willing to listen to a crazy story. By gently questioning Mel, Hilda had discovered enough to track down Beresford's identity. His name was Robert Langdon. His father had been murdered, almost certainly by Luther Szatson, when he discovered that dangerous violations were being intentionally built into the Beresford.

Before the fire, Mel had been a rising star, just beginning to shine. Now she was a mega superstar. Her concert recording had led to three top positions on *Billboard,* her downloads were slowing iTunes, and the checks were beyond belief. Suddenly, they were looking at a seven-figure income. Monthly.

Hilda told herself it wasn't success that made her so grateful to Mel. She finally felt love in its true and unselfish form. In her mind, there had crystallized one thought: make it up to Mel. Give her what she wants.

So now, at last, she was ready. With Mel waiting and the entire world watching, Hilda turned onto the street where the group home was located. Ten carloads of paparazzi followed.

She strode down the block, pushing reporters and camera crews aside. She marched up onto the weathered porch of the big old house, where she was greeted by a hard-faced man backed by two large teenagers and what looked to her like a Great Dane with filed teeth.

"You need to leave him alone. Let him get his bearings."

"I want to hear him tell me that." She shouted, "Beresford, dammit, get out here!"

The manager stepped in front of the door. "Ma'am—"

"Don't you *ma'am* me, little man."

The dog started barking, a series of great, roaring woofs. She glared him down, then stepped across the porch, brushed past them all, and entered the house.

"Beresford! Beresford, it's Mom. Where are you?"

Silence. To her right, there was an empty living room; to her left, a family room where the TV was on. A CNN reporter was yammering into the camera about Melody.

"BERESFORD!"

The manager had come in behind her. "Ma'am, this is private property!"

She marched upstairs and went from bedroom to bedroom.

She found him about where she'd expected to, hiding in the back of a closet with the door closed.

His big eyes looked up at her, full of fear but also the power she'd seen in him before. This was an unusual person, but not a weak one. In fact, he was incredibly strong. This kid had raised himself in the damn walls of a building. He was resourceful and highly intelligent.

"Come on, Robbie," she said gently. "Mel's frantic. We've got to get you back to the hospital."

Three cops came piling into the room. "Excuse me, ma'am," one of them said. "There's been a complaint. I'm afraid—"

Hilda turned and looked up at the cop. Why was everybody else in the world so damn gigantic? Well, shortness hadn't stopped Napoleon, and it wasn't going to stop her.

"Come on, Robbie," she said.

"Ma'am, you can't do this. This boy is an unidentified ward of Los Angeles County."

"Your information is out of date, officer. This boy's name is Robert James Langdon. His parents are dead, and if you call Child Protective Services, you'll find that Hilda Cholworth has been awarded kinship care on the basis of the fact that I'm so damn pushy the judge was afraid to say no." She dragged Beresford out of the closet. "Come on. We're going back to Mel, and don't tell me you're scared because I won't listen."

She didn't say it, but she was scared, too, as she led him out into the mob of journalists.

But the mob scene she was anticipating didn't happen. At least, not at first. This was because the appearance of this tall boy with his otherworldly eyes, rippling muscles, and shining hair simply stunned them to silence.

The press and the public had glimpsed him before but had never seen him up close, and it was an unforgettable experience. His eyes were big, and the way he used them reminded Hilda of the steady gaze of a tiger with the sweetness of a kitten. He was jammed into a T-shirt and jeans, but you could see the rippling athleticism of his muscles. His appearance told you at once that this was no ordinary person—this was somebody very special. If ever you could say there was such a thing as a magical being, that's what he was.

In other words, a perfect fit for her golden daughter.

All at the same moment, the mob of journalists seemed to snap out of the trance. Flashes exploded, questions were shouted, video cameramen backed up before them as they moved toward the car.

The manager stood behind them on the porch with his hands on his hips.

"I'm gonna see Melody again?" Beresford asked.

"You are. In fact, you're gonna see a lot of her. I'm on your side, Robbie."

"Is that my name?"

"You'll remember more in time. You're suffering from something called traumatic amnesia."

"Do you know anything about my dad and mom? Where I lived?"

She was silent, wanting him to be with Mel again first, then later to begin the painful process of remembering his childhood terror. He had lost a lot. He had lost everything. But he'd found love, and that would heal him.

In the hospital, Beresford grew wary. He didn't like elevators, hallways, or crowds.

They came to Melody's room. He went up to the door. Then he turned and gave Mom a questioning look.

"Go ahead."

"She's not busy?"

"You crazy kid, for you she's *never* busy!"

Still he stood there, unsure.

"Oh, fer—" She opened the door and pushed him in, then followed.

Mel lit up and threw her arms toward him, wincing from pain but doing it anyway. Her beloved Beresford bent to her and embraced her, and over his shoulder, Mel's eyes met her mom's. In them, Hilda saw the spark of gratitude that every parent longs to see. They'd fight again, no doubt, but right now the moment was perfect, and for that Hilda was grateful.

She put her plastic cigarette in her mouth and went down to the hospital cafeteria, where she had spent so many hours. She drank a cup of coffee and thought long thoughts of the way life goes, how lovers find each other in all kinds of strange ways.

When she went back upstairs, Mel was asleep in her bed, and Beresford was in the big chair beside her.

Hilda cried a little, watching them in their innocent peace.

Melody stirred, then woke up and held out her hand. Hilda reached for it, but Beresford took it instead.

For a moment, she wanted to push him aside, but she stopped herself.

This was their time, and what might come in their lives and their life together was not her business.

It was a hard thing to accept, but she did. Neither of them noticed her; they were too involved in each other.

But as she left, Melody suddenly broke their embrace.

"Mom, thank you," she said. "You gave us a chance."

"Thank you," Beresford repeated.

Hilda left them to each other, and to the future she could hardly even imagine would be theirs.